Alice Thompson was born and brought up in Edinburgh. She read English at Oxford University and then toured the world in the pop group, The Woodentops. Her novella, *Killing Time*, was published by Penguin in 1991. In 1995 she completed a PhD on Henry James and became writer in residence for the Shetland Isles. *Justine* is her first novel. She is now novelist in residence for St Andrew's University.

JUSTINE

ALICE THOMPSON

To Stephen

A *Virago* Book

Published by Virago Press 1997

First published in Great Britain by
Canongate Books, Edinburgh 1996

Copyright © Alice Thompson 1996

The moral right of the author has been asserted

A CIP catalogue record for this book
is available from the British Library

ISBN 1 86049 306 8

Printed and bound in Great Britain by
Clays Ltd, St Ives plc

Virago
A Division of
Little, Brown and Company (UK)
Brettenham House
Lancaster Place
London WC2E 7EN

Lovers and madmen have such seething brains,
Such shaping fantasies, that apprehend
More than cool reason ever comprehends.
The lunatic, the lover and the poet,
Are of imagination all compact:
One sees more devils than vast hell can hold,
That is the madman, the lover, all as frantic
Sees Helen's beauty in a brow of Egypt:
The poet's in a fine frenzy rolling,
Doth glance from heaven to earth, from earth to heaven,
And as imagination bodies forth
The form of things unknown, the poet's pen
Turns them to shapes and gives to airy nothing
A local habitation and a name.

A Midsummer Night's Dream

The style in which my flat is decorated gives everything away about me. A gift to you which includes the fact that there is something about me that will never be given away, let alone sold for a price. The inner recesses of my flat's interior, the darkened niches velveted burgundy over, and the paintings with their faces set to the walls, hint at an enigmatic character with a taste more perverse than is entirely natural. These rooms are stuffed full of *objets d'art* but the space in which I live also requires the rigour of interpretation.

Interior decoration involves, after all, (and I mean after *all*), the black art of manipulation and the casting of spells. The arabesques on the walls run circles round my visitors' preconceptions of me. The sword of perfect taste is brandished with which to chop off their heads. Now, they are too afraid to come in.

From the day that I was born, beauty surrounded me, embraced me, and picked me up, bloody and screaming, in her arms. She had a face as pale and hard as a pearl and her mouth was congealed from the blood-red drop of a ruby. She took her son home to Blenheim House where I became confused between the symmetry of my mother's form and the arches that carved up the span between the high-ceilinged rooms. This has been my birthright: the indissoluble link between a house and the person who lives in it. To describe my flat to you in detail is to tell you exactly where I stand. It is my way of throwing down the gauntlet.

The drawing-room is covered in deep blue tapestries

which crawl up the walls like the dying waves of the sea. Peacocks of gold strutting down the corridors of a maze are interweaved into its depths. Curtains fall down over the twelve paned windows in impenetrable tresses of green. The thick tangible texture of the room possesses a landscape of its own. It is easy to slip on the mahogany of the wooden floor which is burnished ox-blood. Lilies of the holiest white sprout from a charcoal vase, their sharp green leaves that could cut skin shafting up between the petals. Their decadent scent makes the air heavy, their sweetness sometimes so suffocating it is difficult to breathe.

Plants grow in the bathroom and honeysuckle reaches her arms in through the window. The iron paws of lions stand at each corner of the huge porcelain bath.

The library is from where I am now writing to you, writing out the story of Justine. The shadows on the shelves around me are only books. When I hold up their pages to the light the paper of many of them is so thin that the words of the other side strike backwards, through. From the library steep oaken stairs lead up to my bedroom.

The colours of my bedroom which are in black and gold have an awful symmetry of their own. It is always evening in here for the curtains are perpetually drawn. The candlestick on the bedside table is of a golden serpent, his head raised as if about to strike, a candle flickering in his wide open mouth. He has holes for eyes. I lie on my bed, my arms outstretched in the shape of a cross and realize slowly that I know of all the suffering and joy that the world contains. I can grasp the entirety of the globe in my hands. In the darkness my body hardens into ebony and my eyes transform into ingots of steel.

The meaning of my existence lies within these rooms of mine. My anxieties and ecstasies are framed by their walls. I am protected from the profound nausea and terror that the outer world with its lack of pattern can invoke in me at a touch of its filthy hand. Outside I was so vulnerable, so prone to the malignancy of other people. I needed to screw my courage to the sticking-place to make it to the corner of the square.

TWO

At least children are honest. Years ago, when I once suffered little children to come to me, they shouted out 'cripple' or sniggered behind their tiny hands at the way I walked. Children speak the truth. It was the adults who lied, big, black, spidery lies. They only pretended to avert their eyes. Adults relish perversion of any kind, but a *physical* deviation: what a joy. A fleshy symbol of what is different is the glorious manifestation of sin. When I walked down the streets I became an entertainer, a magician who conjured up silver coins from behind his ears.

As a child I had liked the way the tip of my foot converged into three large toes like the webbed foot of a duck. I had liked the way the skin of my foot, unlike the skin of the rest of my body, was as resilient and hard as the saddle of a horse, but in the space under the arch was as smooth and moist as clay. The limping which was the result of the foreshortened leg, seemed only natural. The rocking movement from side to side as I walked made me feel as if I were gliding not over the ground but over water. However, as I grew older, I began to notice that when my mother bathed me she refused to touch my foot or even turn her head in its direction. It was left to my Nanny to soap and caress the arch, whispering in my ear that I was her little Achilles. When I was fitted with the black platformed shoe, it was the absence of the rocking movement that seemed unnatural. I now had to walk on earth like other people.

As a young boy I used to watch, in secret, my mother dress for dinner. Her beauty besotted me. Standing in the cold of the dark corridor, I would peer into her bedroom out of which warm light and scented skin would pour. She would be sitting, half naked at the mirror, her round full breasts reflected in the glass so that I could feast upon them from every angle. My father would lie on the bed watching her too, but out of sight from where I stood. They would speak desultorily to each other. One evening my father stepped, for the first time, into my line of vision to fasten up a line of pearls around my mother's neck. Like a stranger, he bent down over her powdered skin.

'If only he didn't have such a beautiful face,' she said to him quietly, 'But he has the face of Adonis. If he looked like a troll, it would make more sense. I could accept his deformity more easily. But the flawlessness of his face mocks me. I can hardly bear to look at him.'

It didn't matter that I could not see my father's face for when I could, I was unable to read it – the canvas was blurred and out of focus with the interior man. Sometimes when he was in the room beside me, I had to look at him twice to confirm that he was there. One spring afternoon I watched him, from the top of the stairs, smuggle a painting up into the attic. The painting was wrapped in brown paper so that I could not see what it represented.

4

THREE

My mother worshipped at her mirror's shrine: she adored
beauty and her own was no exception. She would gaze
upon herself for hours and I would watch her gazing.
Idolaters came from all over the country to pay her tri-
bute. They came in the form of men. Their bodies were
dark-skinned and pale, *svelte* and *gauche*, but they all
spoke in the same tongue.

The heat of my thirteenth summer melted the days and
nights together into a cauldron of gold. Time collapsed.
Every morning seemed like a drained-blue memory of
yesterday. At night, as I lay in bed, my window wide
open to the sound of the owl, the heat of the day would
slide insidiously into my bed beside me. The heat of the
day kept me awake with its feverish stroking turning me
from side to side and licking my skin with its hot tongue,
as the moon hung quietly outside in the swollen sky.

One evening, the heat turned me out of my bed,
pushed my naked body out with its hands. It forced me to
run out of the house down to the lake, past the walled
garden. A boat was moored to the small wooden pier.
Rowing out into the centre of the mirrored lake I
anchored over and below the moon. I stood for a moment
balanced on the gunwale of the boat looking out into the
night stillness. I dived. The cold water parted open for
my body only to grab hold of me again in its icy grasp. I
opened my eyes as I plunged down into its blackness, and
it was as if I were flying up into the night sky.

Although I never reached the bottom, now, from the
library where I write, I can imagine what it is like. At the

bottom of the lake are starfish, as if they are stars fallen straight from the sky in the same pattern that they formed above. Rainbow fish dart like fireflies through the transparent water. Scarves of green weeds wave as if undulating in the breeze. At the bottom of the lake, I am sure, is the silent and profound version of what is above. Down there, at the bottom of the lake, just out of my reach.

That evening I surfaced to look out over the water at the white-pillared folly that palely glimmered within the shadows of the other side of the lake. Like a ghost, my mother, in transparent silk, her back turned to me, stood on its wide steps. One of her pilgrims stood beside her, his face reflecting blankly the light of the moon. From the centre of the cool water of the lake, I watched this strange man shut his forget-me-not eyes, as with her mouth she plucked out his heart through his open lips.

FOUR

When my mother aged, she aged inexorably and terribly. She covered the mirrors in Blenheim House in black net veils, as if in mourning for the lost beauty once reflected in them. The flesh that had once clung so tautly to her high cheekbones was pulled off the bone in jowls and lines, by remorseless invisible hands. Age clawed at the corner of her eyes and drew red veins across her face. But it was in the expression of her eyes that the price she was paying showed most.

For every new line that marked her face I added to my rooms an object of art. Kensington Gardens became a memorial to her loveliness. I felt pity for her: I understood about disfigurement.

My own face, however, seemed to grow younger rather than older as the years passed.

'It is not natural,' she said, 'For experience to have marked you so little. It is as if life has not long enough fingers to touch you.'

As my mother's beauty disintegrated, so did her mind. For her sense of identity was dependent on how she appeared. From being dry and elliptical her language metamorphosed into childish anecdote. The grace of her body turned into the forelegs of a seaside donkey. Every time I came to visit her I noticed that another Dresden shepherdess had lost her arm. The black smiling sand-boy that had stood by the side of the main stairs had had his nose knocked off – the white of the chipped porcelain glared out from beneath. Only when every precious art figurine in Blenheim House had lost a limb did I realize that this was not due to my mother's clumsiness. Surgical precision had performed each amputation. She had gone around all the statues in the house, deforming them one by one. After her death I discovered the limbs in a large box marked in red felt-tip pen MISCELLANEOUS, which she had stored under her bed. Inside, piled up high, were legs, teeth, hands and ears, made of china, clay or coloured glass. I wondered if she had kept them there to gloat over, or if one day she had planned to stick the limbs back on. Our family motto had always been FACTA NON VERBA.

FIVE

Beauty is spring-water cold. She doesn't twist and weave and shadows only serve to accentuate her features. Her

7

static opacity is like a mirror which refuses to reflect anything but itself.

My love of beauty is why I collect art. For art renders beauty immortal, traps her for eternity in amber. The painted details of a pure shaft of light, a creamy tuft of ermine fur, a bleeding jewel defy the passing of time. The art I collect must, of course, conform to the ideal. Art that does not is a lower form of life, a form of degradation.

After the thrill of seeing a beautiful object for the first time, my second desire is to possess her. I want to take her home, touch her, lock her up, take her out, look at her, stroke her, whenever I wish. If I had not been born into money, I would have become an art-thief.

Do not dismiss this compulsion to own what is beautiful as superficial, as only a matter of style. For the exquisite sense of pleasure I experience when gazing upon an object of beauty is more profound than any meditation on the nature of truth. You may think, perhaps, that this worship of beauty is dangerously romantic. That I have carved out for myself, within the maelstrom of the twentieth century's final decade, an unnatural vacuum. And you would be right. *For tell me, what is so good about reality?* Would you prefer that I decorated my flat with famine victims, that I laced my floors with leprous skin?

SIX

It is as if I see the years of my life before I met Justine, through the water of a still pond. I collected art and went to dinner parties and talked to elegant, articulate people on a frequent basis whom I had no desire to meet again. I was in control of my life to the point of the absurd. The future had already happened. Yet at night the predictability of my life began to be disturbed by the recurrence of a single dream.

I am driving up a wide avenue lined at regular intervals by tall beeches. The silver light of their leaves is reflecting the blueness of the sky. The hot afternoon is being bled dry by the scarlet rhododendrons which flourish between the trees. I didn't think that I had a destination.

It is only when I turn the corner of the avenue that I see the house. A huge Gothic house rears up in front of me like a leviathan raising its head out of the sea. Its skin is of dark grey stone. Gargoyles, grinning and gulping, with wide open mouths line its side. One of the gutters has broken and water trickles down in a line over the surface of its body eroding the greyness to reveal the white chalkiness beneath. Seeing the water, I realize that, in spite of the heat, it has only recently stopped raining. The sky behind its frame is of unlimited blue: unreally, as if a sheet of azure cellophane has been inserted behind the façade of the house. The flatness of the sky contrasts with the thick three-dimensionality of the house. To the right of the house grows a maze of dark green yew, standing taller than a man. In the dream I never reach the house, I always wake up just as I am turning the corner of the avenue and seeing the house for the first time.

Waking, I would lie outstretched on the horse-hair sofa, the disturbing memory of the dream diffusing in the lilac spirals of the opium I would occasionally smoke. It was through the sweetness of this smoke that the portrait, which hung above the swirling marble of the mantelpiece, invariably drew my eye.

SEVEN

The portrait was a full-length figure of a woman. She was sitting at a table, in a bare dark room with a window whose bars flung their shadows across the left-hand side of her face. On the table lay an open book and a bottle of ink. The writing inside the book was hand-written, not printed, in childish form. The script covered half a page. The actual words, however, were illegible. In her hand she held a fountain pen. A velvet dress clung to the contours of her body, her breasts offering themselves up to the viewer by the low cut of its Empire line.

Her hard pale eyes, set wide apart in her face, contained the knowledge that nothing was of any consequence outside of how she looked. Her gaze did not look directly at me, but coyly, to one side. This meant I could look at her to my heart's content. By looking away she put herself even more on display to me. This oblique sacrifice of herself sealed my love.

In the half-state of consciousness that smoking opium induced in me, I could look at this portrait with contentment for the entire day until evening fell and she would turn her head towards me and smile. The background of the picture would change also. Instead of sitting in the shadowy room she would be sitting in a formal garden. Just to the right of her would stand a line of yew trees which I could see, on closer inspection, formed the side of a maze. What never changed about the picture, no matter how many times I looked at it, was the plaque on the lower edge of its gilt frame which read *Justine*.

This was how I spent the last days of my life until my

mother's death. Interior, self-reflexive days where the source of all my pleasure were my day and night dreams. Drugs and absolute solitude gave me ultimate control over my life. My solipsistic universe could never stray from the strictures that I set it.

EIGHT

On the day that I discovered my mother's body I had driven up to Blenheim House, one early summer afternoon, for tea. For the past year my mother, in spite of being physically fit, had taken to her bed. It was her way of hiding from the world. She could no longer bear the gaze of others. However, her self-confinement had weakened her. What had started off as a gesture had become an ending in itself.

That Sunday afternoon it was raining outside as I made my way down the lonely corridors of the house that I had once played in as a child. I softly knocked on the same bedroom door through which I had used to watch my mother dressing for dinner. As there was no reply I assumed that she had fallen asleep and I opened the door and entered. But her unmade bed was empty, the sheets trailing on the floor. I could hear behind the closed door of the adjoining bathroom, the slow relentless sound of a tap dripping. Walking up to the door I noticed that the carpet beneath my feet was damp and soft like moss. Water was seeping from underneath the bathroom door. I turned the handle of the door and it opened easily.

The naked body of my mother lay in the overflowing bath. What shocked me more than the fact that she was dead was the extent to which her body had been ruined by age. When I had last seen her naked the fullness and suppleness of her flesh reflected in her mirror had entranced me. Now her breasts were slack and pendulous. Varicose veins scoured her legs, like purple buds about to burst into bloom. The shape of her body was concealed by roll upon roll of fat. Blood spiralled into the water in arabesques from her swollen split wrists. The make-up that she had so carefully applied to her face before cutting her wrists had smeared. Mascara ran down her cheeks in black lines like the bars of a cage.

I bent down over her and carefully lifted her body out of the bath. I carried her out into the bedroom where I placed her as gently as I could onto the bed. I dried her body and wiped the remaining make-up from her face. But this revealed the second mask of her age-ravaged skin. With the aid of her make-up, I tried, as she had tried, to restore back to the face some of its youth and beauty. I tried to paint the blood back into her lips and the blush of life back into her cheeks. In vain I tried to repair the damage of mortality.

Evening had fallen by the time I walked back out through the house. I passed by the various statues and figurines, with their absent limbs, that stood about the rooms. One by one I knocked them down, hearing them crash to the floor behind me. They broke into such tiny pieces, which scattered across the floor, that mending them would have proved impossible.

NINE

My flat seemed cool and at peace as I entered it later that same night. I lay down on the sofa and took out my opium pipe. It was of ivory, ornately carved with wood-land animals. Deer and squirrels leapt and clambered over its stem. The pipe had been bought purely for aesthetic reasons, for its intricate decoration, and I had only begun to use it for its original purpose after I had started to handle it and realized that its patterns demanded to be read. The pleasure of using the pipe became entwined with the pleasure of the drug until the two became indistin-guishable: just as the figures of the leaping deer were inseparable from the actual structure of the pipe.

The sweet taste of the opium was pleasantly nauseous and my gaze fell inevitably on to the portrait of Justine. To my shock a change had come over her expression: the consolatory quality of her beauty had disappeared. Her face had grown malevolent, her eyes had narrowed, and the book that she had been writing had fallen to the floor as if she were no longer interested in the mere construc-tion of words. I had the strong impression that she was angry that she was still trapped inside the room and that her painted background had not been transformed into the garden where she preferred to sit. I shut my eyes to block out her anger that seemed directly aimed at me. When I opened them she had returned to her normal pos-ture, serene and self-contained, her eyes looking off to one side. However, after this incident I perceived a dis-tinctly erotic edge to her beauty which had not been there before.

TEN

Looking back now, I see that it was only natural that I should first meet Justine at a funeral. Justine and Death had a natural affinity for each other: they followed each other around. Her icy demeanour enticingly challenged the warm and passionate breath of death. Death, as soon as he laid eyes upon her, would have wanted his way with her. It was just that Justine played hard to get.

At the altar, my mother lay in the open coffin surrounded by the whiteness of lilies. Her ruined beauty now lay on display to the world. The service was simple and apart from the Priest there were only three people at the funeral: myself, my mother's maid and a woman who was standing three rows in front, her back turned to me. She was wearing a dress which was cut low at the back so that I could see the sinuous muscles that twisted like snakes under her skin. Often now, when I think of Justine, it is of her back, of her turning away from me, walking away. Her back is the place from where it is always safe to watch. She was sheathed in beige silk, the colour of shadowed snow. Even from the back I could tell that she would cost me too much.

The arches of the Norman church that we stood beneath reproduced in their fluid form the curve of her shoulder. The combination of proportion and grace which was the architecture of the church, also formed the body of the woman. I still had not seen her face and as I waited for a glimpse of it I fantasized the various ways in which the bones might be sculptured. However, I had no doubt in my mind that her face would be devastating, that she would in one pure way devastate me.

The stone of the church was pale gold, like her hair, and light shone through the blood-red of the stained glass, casting shadows on both. The church smelt of dust.

Only when the coffin was carried down the aisle by the bearers, did I catch a glimpse of her face as she turned to look at it. It was Justine. The face of my painting had been brought to life in front of me. The image had been made flesh. Except the flesh of this Justine was chiselled out of ice. No facial expression disfigured the Madonna-like purity of her face. The look as she followed with her eyes my mother's coffin down the aisle had the indifferent but focused attention of a child. In the moment of recognition this stranger had been frozen into my heart. As soon as I saw her, I wanted her for my own. To place her in my flat in the best position for the light.

Suddenly the atmosphere of the church changed. The dusty light and archaic space grew distant and two-dimensional, as if they were existing only to form the background to my vision of Justine. Justine's smooth curved body gradually, as I watched it, grew huge until her shoulders fitted into the arches of the church, her face still retaining its look of acute centredness. Until someone tapped me on my shoulder and said my name. I turned around. It was my mother's maid, Alice, looking up at me with puppy-brown eyes. Tears were pouring down her wrinkled face.

'I'm so sorry, Sir,' she said, 'So very sorry'.

I think now of my mother buried beneath the ground. She lives on but only in the unreliable memory of those who still mourn her. Her image has been lost to the vagaries of life.

Immediately after the funeral I looked around in vain for Justine but she had disappeared. I returned to the church but it was empty, except for the lilies, and as I looked around its perpendicular space, the building turned banal, became a carapace of stone, like the empty shell of a snail. There was too much room here for God.

ELEVEN

One day my solitude had been enough to content me. The next, a door had opened off to its side and I had walked straight through into a void. The vision of Justine had made the difference. In other ways my life, on the surface, remained the same. The artefacts of my choice still stood around me. Creamy marble boys and ebony heads continued in their silent observation of me. However, the knowledge of Justine was with me now and it stuck to my life like a shadow.

The height of summer had arrived with a vengeance. The central private gardens of my square dried up over night, the grass turning to the colour of her hair. Half-naked children stumbled over the spiky grass like those bottom-heavy leaded toys that always return to the upward position, whatever happens.

Justine was not there, everywhere I looked. Her absence paralysed my flat, paralysed the air, paralysed the point to living. Trees turned black, as if charred by the night. I could not comprehend the power that one sighting of her had had over me except to explain it in terms of my Destiny. The portrait of Justine had come to life: the vulgarity of a simple coincidence could not explain it away.

Once I had seen her, there was no longer any alternative. Other women became impostors. Walking down the street I recognized the back of her head often, her hair glinting like the gold of a Byzantine mosaic. But the face was never hers — it was scared and hooked, dumb and malleable, or petulant and conceited. These faces had stolen her hair to frame their own expressions. When I saw what these strangers had done, appropriated part of her beauty for themselves, I wanted to reclaim her locks, slash them off with a sharp blade, carry the sashes of her hair home. The thieves of Justine's hair should have been punished. These women should not have been allowed to walk down the streets bearing their booty, exhibiting their lush tresses, letting it fall down their slender backs, Justine's hair.

However, even worse was the impudent theft of her face. These strange women wore her face like a mask, but I saw that they had even prised out her eyes, the exact shade of jade, and placed them like precious stones into the rings of their own sockets. And in horror, I imagined her, the blank where her face used to be, the serrated edges of flesh, encircling her high forehead, chin and jaw where the skin, the soft white skin that had once been Justine's skin, had been pulled away to reveal the structure of the bone beneath.

Sometimes it was only her gestures that were appropriated. A woman put her hand to the back of her neck in thought. These gestures had been snatched from Justine and used by strangers promiscuously in the street. My resentment turned to pity for it was in ignorance that these women performed these impersonations of Justine. They were puppets going through the motions, vehicles for the true justification of their existence, of the beating of their hearts, which was that they lived as clues, traces, bodily mementos of Justine.

TWELVE

In Justine's eyes I had drawn breath only for a moment.
She had seen me once and turned away. Her life was now
continuing effortlessly, gratifyingly, without me. She did
not need me to watch her in order to turn the pages of a
new book, she did not need me to watch her in order to
undress garment by silken pastel garment. I was not
necessary for the graceful movements that she made. She
would be able to touch herself without knowledge of my
name, without the image of me in her thoughts. She did
not know that in reality she needed me in order to exist,
that without the concentration of my thoughts she was
just a phantom. It was something that I would have to
teach her. But until then I could always take her in my
dreams behind her back.

To explain to you the intensity of my longing seems an
impossible act, but it is what the story of Justine is about.
The story is the writing out of my desire: there is no
other motivation, neither of intellect nor of revenge.
They came later (or before I now write). Justine was the
location of my desire, she had trapped it inside her body.
It was up to me to track it back down.

I did not know under what circumstances I would see
her again. But I knew that I would. Now that I had seen
her in the flesh there was no other possibility. By the first
time I had seen her, it was already too late.

THIRTEEN

The next Sunday after my mother's funeral, I decided to
pay a visit to the National Gallery, in Trafalgar Square.

The permanence of the art inside, I thought, would demolish any notion of the mortality of beauty. The afternoon was warm and heady and the cool air and the presence of such exquisite paintings in the gallery's interior did indeed offer consolation. The high arches of the pale grey rooms of the Sainsbury Wing reminded me of the church I had been in the week before. My obsession with Justine had become less highly charged, had calmed down. But due only to the premonition that I would inevitably see her again.

I turned the corner into the final west room of the wing. It was where one of my favourite paintings of the gallery hung: Uccello's *St. George and the Dragon*. A woman was standing in front of it, staring at it, absorbed. It was Justine.

I continued to observe her, unseen, from the entrance of the room. But there was something imperceptibly different about her. In the church she had exuded a sublime self-confidence. Here in the gallery, she was standing in a less poised manner, her back hunched, as if, as she stared at the painting, she was afraid that the dragon might break free. Afraid that it would make a sudden, unprovoked attack upon her. The painting's triangular relationship of man, woman and monster seemed to be crunching up her posture as I watched.

Her whole appearance was dishevelled and incoherent. Her dress was covered in a grotesque pattern of flying birds. Her face had lost its alabaster effect that I had noticed in the church. But I was so overcome by seeing her again, that I did not dwell on these superficial changes to her demeanour. Rather, I could not look at her and breathe at the same time.

FOURTEEN

The dove-grey walls behind Justine formed a backdrop to her gilt hair. The golden sheen of the Madonna's clothes in the Byzantine paintings all around us picked up her hair's colour and scattered it across the room. Justine was in relief: her profile was as clear cut as when I had last seen it in the church, as if the edge of her profile had been cut out of black paper and her face made up of the white space that remained.

I crossed the empty room towards her and stood just to the left of her in front of the painting. Engrossed by the painting, she did not even register my presence. Any nervousness I had was dispelled by my sense that Fate was acting on my behalf. Fate began to propel my next moves, regardless of my will. I deliberately caught her eye, but for all the recognition she showed me, I might as well have been a total stranger. To my horror Justine then proceeded to move away from the painting. Words now had become my only option but they stuck in my throat like stones. I had to gag them out.

'We've met before,' I said to her retreating back.

She looked tentatively over her shoulder. I had the uncanny sensation that my words were even truer than they appeared, that I had seen her before somewhere, outside of the church, outside of her similarity to the portrait of Justine.

'I don't think so.' If she had noticed I was a cripple her expression didn't betray it. Her eyes didn't flicker from my face.

'Yes we have. At my mother's funeral, last Sunday. I

saw you in the church.'

'You are making a mistake. Last Sunday I was spending the day in the country. Where I have a house.' I looked at her in disbelief. The expression on her face suddenly indefinably changed. Then she said, as if she had said it a hundred times before,

'You're talking about Justine.'

'Yes,' I said. 'You.'

'No. Not me. My sister. My identical twin.'

I was so taken aback that she was not Justine, that the further act of fate that not only did Justine share the face of the painting but also its name passed me by.

Justine's sister walked back and stood next to me in front of the Uccello.

'"And he lay hold on the dragon, that odd serpent, which is the Devil, and Satan, and bound him a thousand years." Milton. Don't you find dragons fascinating? The way man has made them up only so he can go round slaughtering them. But I don't think he's made them up altogether. I believe in them too.' She clapped her hands together and laughed.

She was quite clearly insane.

'I'm always on the look out for a dragon,' I said. 'The reward for killing one is so immense.'

'A beautiful princess?'

'A beautiful princess.' I smiled at her.

'I'm Juliette.' She repeated it, as if she were afraid that I might forget her name. 'Juliette. It doesn't pay to get us confused.' She had a smudge of red paint on her cheek near her left ear, that looked like blood.

'You have to admit it's a coincidence,' I said, 'To have

bumped into you so quickly after meeting Justine for the first time.'

'No. I don't.' She smiled again. I didn't know what to make of this. Did she, like me, not believe in coincidences?

She seemed direct, so I thought I would try a more direct approach.

'You have an unforgettable face.'

The expression on her face changed frighteningly quickly, a cloud of resentment covered it, black and turgid.

'You mean *Justine* has an unforgettable face.'

The differences between the two sister were becoming more and more noticeable the longer I spent with Juliette. Juliette's expressions were flung onto her face more thoughtlessly and erratically than Justine's. Juliette's smile had the charm of complication and her hair, when she moved her head, gave off the smell of burning wood. She had a disarming smile – a sure sign of neurosis. The charming always depend on the resources of desperation. The image of Justine I had imprinted onto Juliette's face was being gradually effaced by Juliette's child-like movements and disturbed sexuality. Juliette, I ascertained quickly, would believe in the best in people, look for the best in the worst of men. Juliette believed in fairy tales.

However, I wondered secretly if her role as child-woman was a part that she played rather than had thrust upon her. Her nervous fragility seemed almost too blatant to be realistic. But perhaps, I reasoned, it was simply because the contrast between her manner and Justine's was so great that the identity of Juliette somehow ended up spurious.

I pointed back to the painting. 'I like so much the way

the painting which is about such primitive themes as desire and death and myth is constructed with such elaborate control.'

At least, I think that is what I said. As far as I can remember, the beginning of my seduction of Justine's sister began with those words. However, I may have said something completely different – memory is so unreliable. Who can tell? It is too late to tell – except for me. Juliette has long since gone. I will always have the last word. There is no ghost in *this* machine.

FIFTEEN

That same afternoon Juliette and I went for tea in the gallery. As we walked together through the rooms of paintings down the wide stone steps to the tea-room, I had to stop my hands trembling from the excitement of it all. At one point I almost stumbled and Juliette reached out her hand to stop me from falling. Her fingers, as long and as slender as Justine's, held on to my hand for longer than was strictly necessary. I saw the image of Justine cross her face briefly and then dissipate into the cool dusty atmosphere of the gallery.

As we drank tea, I continued to observe Juliette closely. Her leaf-green eyes seemed translucent, as if perpetually wet from tears. Her eyes had an open expression as if sending out a general invitation to be hurt. Simultaneously her gaze went in on itself, exhibiting that she had an interior world without betraying its contents. On the occasions that I glimpsed Justine in Juliette's face, Justine would at once turn her back to me and walk away.

Juliette sat like a child, her legs together and her hands

23

tightly clasped. Her body language was like that of an infant. But also, like a child, she would have the odd moment of utter unselfconsciousness where she would suddenly splay her legs wide open and I could see straight up to her centre between her white shadowy thighs. Her mouth was tremulous and soft as a ripe pear that had just been sliced open.

We walked slowly out into the hot light of Trafalgar Square. We said goodbye with the pigeons fluttering at our feet. The sun was dying behind Nelson's head. She wrote her phone number on my hand in large unformed handwriting. I watched her walk away slightly stooped, as if scared that the tall handsome buildings of London were about to collapse on top of her.

Exhausted but excited I took a taxi back to Kensington Gardens. Some of my mother's possessions now stood around me, an African mask hung on the wall and a silver Chinese Mandarin stood on the rosewood side table. Everything else, broken or otherwise, remained under the dust sheets in Blenheim House.

SIXTEEN

It was already almost dark when Juliette and I came out of the cinema. Juliette was wearing, on our first date together, a thick cotton dress covered in purple stars and white moons; she reminded me slightly of a pantomime witch. Her hair was loose and tangled. The faces of the other people in the audience who were crowding around us at the exit, looked half dead as the light of the real world first hit them. We had just been to see the rescreening of Alfred Hitchcock's *Vertigo*.

'I know a place where we can eat,' she said as we stood stationary amongst the walking dead.

She led me back into the centre of London from the South Bank, over Hungerford Bridge. St. Paul's was lit up by a blue light like an architect's painted model and the buildings overlooking the river had the appearance of a theatrical façade. Stopping in the middle of the bridge, we looked down over the dark waters of the Thames, dense and fluid with its own deep currents. The lights of the city of London shone across it, emphasizing the force of the water's movement.

Juliette stood with her back to the barrier, her elbows propped up on the edge behind her. A train hurtled by, its noise shattering the unreality of our view. With a sudden lithe movement she pushed down on her arms to hoist herself up on to the narrow ledge.

'Don't do that,' I said. 'It's dangerous. You might fall backwards.'

'You're not scared of heights are you?' she taunted.

She proceeded to bring her feet up on to the top of the barrier and stand up on it, still facing inwards on to the footpath. Her hair was blowing all around her. I could see her teeth smiling between the strands.

'It's so easy to play with death. Tickle it under its arm-pits until it squeals with laughter. I could just jump. Or, if you like, you could push me. Death depends on the smallest of gestures.'

She outstretched her hands to me and I gratefully took hold of them so that I could bring her down.

'Hold tight,' she said.

She stepped backwards off the barrier into the space

that hung hundreds of feet above the wrestling river. She hung for a moment dangling from my arms. She had now let go of my hands altogether: I was holding hers.

She smiled up at me between the bars of the barrier that separated us.

'If you wanted, you could let go.' Her face looked calm. It was mine, I imagined, that looked tortured.

Summoning my strength I hoisted her back over the barrier. We stood facing each other on the bridge.

'That was an incredibly stupid thing to do,' I said.

But without replying she turned on her heels. I followed her across the bridge on to the Embankment. She was now walking with alacrity, as if being chased by an invisible demon snapping at her ankles.

We walked up Charing Cross Road into Soho. Unlike me, she was obviously used to London on foot, used to its narrow crannies and ungiving crowds. Up until now, I had only experienced London (only experienced this *century*), at a safe and privileged distance. Juliette then turned off Old Compton Street into a dark street full of scaffolding. I could see no sign of a restaurant at all, just tall terraced houses fronted by narrow entrances with entry systems to them marked by names such as APHRO- DITE or DIANA. The rooms on the above floors were suffused by red light where these goddess-whores turned men into trees or deer.

The garish lettering of the café's name only became visible when we were standing directly beneath it. The flashing sign written in green neon light, THE LORELEI, had been concealed by the metal scaffolding. I followed Juliette up some shallow stone steps into a small room.

The light was dim except for the flickering of candles on the checked tablecloths. Home-made wooden tables dotted the room. Covering one side of the wall was a painted mural. The painting was of the Lorelei on a rock, naked, her marigold hair falling over her breasts. A ship in the distance, far out to sea, was sailing in her direction. She was luring the ship to her doom with her voice. But I am safe, I thought, because I can't hear her singing.

SEVENTEEN

As we sat down Juliette pointed to the mural and asked me if I liked it.

'It of course depicts a truth – the extraordinary power of women over men. Women are without question the more dangerous sex,' I replied.

Juliette was now looking at me in a particularly unthreatening way. She looked about as dangerous as a dormouse.

'Oh, but you're wrong,' she said. 'Men *make* women dangerous.'

Did she mean 'make' as in make up or 'make' as in incite? I really couldn't be bothered with her riddles. I was just about to change the subject when my elbow grazed against my glass of red wine and knocked it over. The table cloth was soaked and we had to move to another table.

We talked for an hour or so while eating a bland, unappetizing pasta, but I managed to learn little about her or Justine.

'Whose funeral was Justine at?' she asked.

'My mother's.' I expected the standard response of sympathy but she said nothing.

'What was she like?' she asked.

'Beautiful' I replied.

'I don't mean Justine.'

'Neither do I.'

'And?'

'And? What else do you need to know? Isn't a woman being beautiful enough for you, enough for anyone?'

Juliette looked down at the table and I tried to read her face. Seven different emotions seem to cross her face at the same time, not one of them I could distinctly interpret. This was why Juliette could never be beautiful: too many emotions ran cross-current in her. She lacked the severe implacability whose *raison d'etre* was to be ruffled by desire. Juliette had too much character in her face to allow a lover room to leave his mark. Her countenance left nothing for him to do. Far better the *tabula rasa*, the divine blankness of a Justine, that begged me to write all over her.

EIGHTEEN

I walked Juliette home. She lived in Waterloo, above a pet shop, down a gloomy street called The Cut. The street was deserted and the moon shone high and round in the starless sky.

'The moon always makes me want to take risks,' Juliette said.

She was standing on the doorstep of the pet shop. Litter fluttered beneath her feet and the smell of rotten vegetables emanated up from the street. Out of the blue, a newspaper article I had recently read came to mind. An animal behaviourist had wanted to find out the most effective way of winning an animal's love. He constructed an experiment involving three puppies. The first puppy he showered with affection, the second he consistently verbally and physically abused and the third was treated on alternative days with both methods. At the end of the experiment it was the third puppy who ended up most devoted to him. The insecurity of being treated so inconsistently triggered off the third puppy's need to please. Juliette was to be my third puppy. I was serious about winning her love. She looked up at me and, in the doorway's shadow, her face could have belonged to Justine. I bent down and kissed her mouth. However, it was the face of Juliette who turned away from me a few moments later.

In the background the tannoy of Waterloo Station was announcing the times and destinations of the trains running out of London. The rhythm and intonation sounded like the chanting of a litany. In the grey empty street it had started to rain, drops falling down over Juliette's face. In the blue light from the fish tank in the pet shop window she looked like a sorceress.

'I'll get you an umbrella,' she suddenly said.

Before I could stop her, she had disappeared inside the pet shop and shut the door. The light in the floor above the shop went on and I saw her silhouette move about the rooms that faced on to The Cut. The door opened again and she reappeared on to the street. Handing over the umbrella without a word, she went back in and shut the door behind her.

The design of the umbrella was hideous and having opened it up, I had to shut it again at once. I was unable to find a taxi and finally had to walk home. I arrived home aching and drenched to the skin.

NINETEEN

I waited a fortnight before phoning Juliette again. Mainly because of a bad cold that I had caught, but also because it gave me a certain pleasure to think that she would be waiting in for my call. As far as I could tell, there was nothing to fill up her thoughts but a kind of waiting for her Prince to come. Just *existing* is never enough for anyone. So I was surprised that when I did phone there was no reply. I phoned consistently over the following few days but still there was no answer. On late Sunday evening I finally got through to her. She recognized my voice immediately, which I took to be a good sign, and she eagerly accepted my invitation to supper the next day.

By eight o'clock I had drawn the curtains and lit the candles and watched the fingers of the flickering flames point their way up to heaven. In the candlelight the portrait of Justine grew increasingly enigmatic. She was watching everything I did, including the premeditated seduction of her sister. It was the fact that it was about to happen in her presence that made it morally right: Justine sanctified it.

The doorbell rang. I heard Juliette say her name in her soft and placatory voice over the intercom. In a moment I was letting her into my flat and the symptoms of nervousness and anticipation that she noticed in me were not altogether feigned.

Juliette sat down on the sofa. She had not seen the portrait of Justine hanging above the mantelpiece directly opposite her. She was too busy looking anxiously about the rest of the room, as if I were about to kidnap her and imprison her in it for the rest of her life.

The patterns on her dress this evening were of apple trees. What made her so frightened, I wondered, of a simple, coherent design? The trees were planted all over the material, their branches intertwining with each other to create an intricate lace-like pattern. The apples were almost hidden by the leaves.

'May I open the window?' she asked.

As she pushed up the window, the cool breeze of the night air gushed into the room between the fluttering curtains.

It was the noise I heard first, a loud angry sound like the beating of flames and then I saw what looked like an open book being violently hurled from one side of the room to the other. The whole room suddenly burst into life with movement. A starling had flown in through the window. The bird dashed about the drawing-room, flying headlong into the mantelpiece, the walls, the portrait, perching momentarily on the sofa before thrusting itself up into the air again.

Unexpectedly, Juliette didn't utter a word or a cry. She stood up, and keeping as still as a statue, held out her arm. Moments later the starling had landed on her outstretched hand, as if she were just another European ornament. Quickly, she brought her other hand down over the bird, trapping it within the cage of her fingers. The bird fluttered hopelessly against its human bars. Transferring the bird to the tight grasp of a single hand, with the other hand, Juliette began gently to stroke the bird's neck. The bird's soft feathers gleamed in a rainbow of colours but its eyes were black with panic. She then with her second finger and thumb ringed its throat for a second, as if she were going to snap its neck, kill it with the fine slim fingers that belonged to Justine. But instead she walked over to the open window and opening up her hand let the starling fly out into the night air of London.

'I hate seeing things imprisoned,' she said.

As if her words were an unconscious directive, I looked at her intent interior face and suddenly spontaneously identified her with the bird. I simultaneously realized that it was not her *fear* of imprisonment speaking, but her *desire for it*. She wanted to be clasped in someone else's hand. Her only way of living in the world was to be locked up inside it. Imprisonment was a form of rescue for her.

'Would *you* mind being imprisoned?' she asked me.

I was taken aback — I had not considered the idea in relation to myself.

'Appalling idea. I wouldn't be able to go to art exhibitions,' I quickly said.

'But you have your own exhibition here. Your own private collection of art. I think you would be quite happy to remain in one or two rooms for the rest of your life, as long as you had your artefacts around you.'

I tried to hide my unease in a slightly disjointed smile. I also attempted to get back a sense of control. In order to do so, I pretended that I had a ventriloquist's doll, not a woman, sitting in my drawing-room. I was unconsciously throwing my voice into her. Without understanding how I was doing it, I was somehow pulling her strings, making her talk, crossing her legs at my will.

Over supper I decided to ask Juliette what she did for a living and later, subtly, when the time was right, probe her for more intimate details about Justine.

'I write. I hardly make a living.'

'What about?'

'It's a kind of autobiography.'

'But you're so young. Nothing much can have happened to you.'

'Things are happening to me all the time. Besides, I'm older than I look.' She smiled.

I tried to get her on to the subject of Justine but she kept on returning to the subject of my mother which seemed to preoccupy her.

'How did your mother die?' she asked.

'She committed suicide.'

'Out of loneliness?'

'No. Because she couldn't bear to grow old.'

I was beginning to resent the directness of her questions, but to get what I wanted from her, I felt I had to answer them politely. It was nearing midnight and I had to find a way of making her stay.

TWENTY

Midnight came and went and Juliette's behaviour began to change. She is a sorceress, I thought, dictated to by the fullness of the moon. She brushed up against me as we passed in the room so that I could smell her perfumed skin. She stroked Lethe, my Burmese cat, until the cat's fur shimmered like moonlight and her back arched voluptuously. Juliette drank glass after glass of Corvo, as if it were water. Did she have any idea at all as to what was inside my head, the double-dealing of my plot? My motivations were hard set and wrapped up in my mind like gifts hidden in a cupboard.

As the carriage clock chimed one, Juliette curled up on the sofa, her dress falling back over her thighs, the flesh of her legs above her stockings as smooth as Venetian glass. Her manner had shed its nubile *gaucherie*, as if it had been invaded by an occult force that had incorrigibly transformed her identity.

I sat down beside her, close, and she didn't flinch. Lethe, however, leapt from her lap. I bent down towards Juliette, raised up her chin gently with my hand, and kissed her. Her soft mouth opened for mine. But suddenly she drew back and sat up. I expected her face to be flushed with desire but instead it looked quiet and reflective.

'Why are you doing this?' she asked, in a matter-of-fact tone.

I tried to control my sense of panic that she had guessed my real reasons.

'Why are you so intent on seducing me?' she continued. 'It would be an obvious to an idiot that you despise me. And find me physically vaguely repulsive. But you are acting as if driven by the devil himself.'

I clutched desperately around in my head for an answer that might satisfy her, appease her insecurity.

'I don't understand how you can say that,' I replied. 'You are completely mistaken. I find you incredibly attractive.'

I leant towards her again and started to play deliberately absentmindedly with a strand of her hair. She turned her head towards me but her eyes were lowered.

'I'm sorry,' she said. 'Ignore me. Writers have such terrible imaginations.'

She raised up her face to be kissed and we began to play out that silent language which has its own grammar. The portrait of Justine watched the proceedings from above the mantelpiece, a smile flickering about her lips in the candlelight. She's smiling at me, I thought, smiling at what I will do for her.

TWENTY-ONE

I woke up the next morning to find that the bedclothes had fallen off us during the night. Juliette was lying next to me, looking up into my eyes. Already I was picking up on a change in her since we had had sex. She was beginning to smell of need. The need of a woman was rotten at the core, it seeped through her whole body, permeated its edges: need spread. It would start in the eyes, make its way through the posture, interfere with the vocabulary, and finally invaded what was once a sensibility. Need provoked the worst crime of all: self-consciousness. Already I could see that what lay beyond Juliette's desperation, her clumsiness, her seriousness, was her encroaching self-consciousness. It crippled her identity, deformed it, crystallized and then shattered it. She was like a cracked mirror, always self-reflecting an image that was deformed.

Juliette sat up and crawled to the end of the bed. Kneeling over my body, she began cradling my right foot in her hands. I watched her face, curious about her reaction to the foot's deformity. However, her mien remained impassive and unreadable. She was tracing the line of the foot's bony deformation as if it were a seashell that she had picked up from the shore.

'You can keep it, if you like,' I said.

She laughed. 'You don't accept it, do you? The asymmetry of your body.'

'No,' I replied. 'It's a misrepresentation.'

Juliette left later that morning. I watched her from my window run down the street. I lay down on my sofa and took out my pipe. Through the myth-making of its smoke the portrait of Justine had changed shape yet again. Her mouth was now wide open and her laughter sounded wicked.

TWENTY-TWO

I had not wanted to return to Waterloo. I had had enough glimpses into the sordidity of Juliette's lifestyle, just from the outside, to last me. However, she had insisted that it was her turn to entertain. And I knew in my heart that I had to see her again. She answered the door to the pet shop in a dress splattered with sepia details (taken from Botticelli's *The Birth of Venus*) of the goddess emerging from the sea in her shell. Juliette was just another impostor, I thought, of a different kind. Icons of love could only be worn by Justine.

I followed her reluctantly through the deserted pet shop. I could hear the animals quietly stirring in their cages. The staircase up to her flat, at the back of the shop, was narrow and steep and covered in a thick coarse carpet, the colour of dense mud. As I followed her up the stairs, a parrot in one of the cages from down below called up, 'Silly Boy ... Silly Boy'.

The plain white door at the top of the stairs had a smooth surface, empty of a number or letter. Juliette inserted her key into the small keyhole which was surprisingly low down in the door. The door was positioned very near the edge of the top step, making it awkward for me to get into her flat without stumbling, but Juliette took my hand.

The hallway was dark inside, but as I followed Juliette down the narrow corridor, I could just make out that the walls were papered in dark red flock. She opened a door at the far end of the passageway. Entering, it took me a while, because of the very dim light, to work out where I was. But as my eyes grew accustomed to the light, I slowly realized that I was standing in the middle of a pile of junk. I was surrounded by *rubbish*. Discarded mannequins, stuffed one-eyed owls, biscuit tins, old torn newspapers, and a stoat perched forever on a tree stump in an old glass case, lay all around. Was this some kind of joke? There was hardly enough space for my feet. Books, hand-written manuscripts, crusts of bread, broken-open piggy-banks and soiled underwear littered the ground. It was as if every conceivable used object in the world was lying on her floor. Worst of all, this room was lived in by a woman. There was not a single trace of feminine tidiness or nicety.

In the distance, in a neighbouring flat, someone had started to play hesitantly on the piano, 'You are my sunshine, my only sunshine'. I looked up at Juliette. She was now standing on the other side of the room, having quickly negotiated all the obstacles in her way with nimble feet. She was staring at me. In the dark saturated room

I watched as she began to move her hands over the sepia print of the dress, stopping at her breasts to touch her nipples, or rubbing between her legs, the material crunching up wetly between her body. Her face was flushed and her mouth open, but her eyes did not leave mine once. The background noise of the chaos, the darkness, the warm smells, the inane tinkling of the piano were all insanely contributing to my heightening arousal.

I was oblivious to the broken chairs and pieces of glass that snatched and cut at my ankles, as I made my way over to her. Reaching out to her, I pulled her body to me, at the same time kissing the warm pale skin of her neck, tearing at her dress to kiss between her breasts, placing my hand between her soft open legs. My desire for her was making it difficult for me to breathe. Without undressing I took her standing up against the off-white peeling walls.

But afterwards, as I belted up my trousers again, I felt ashamed. Juliette torn and dishevelled, stood quietly watching me, her back still leaning against the wall. I felt degraded: for a moment my desire for Juliette had actually been real. I wanted to hit Juliette for what she had done, for her repugnant temptations, for being too much. For making me betray Justine.

I looked around the room again – who could live in a room like this? What sort of person? The debris, the lack of order, the smell, the constant assault to every civilized sense. It would require a kind of insanity or autism to tolerate it. Someone who lived only in the interior world of the mind.

A piece of handwritten manuscript lying on the floor

caught my eye. I picked it up. The page was headed with the single word: PLOT. A diagram of a square had been drawn underneath. At each of the square's corners had been written a name: Juliette, Justine, Jack, and my own. Who was Jack? Juliette snatched the paper from me.

'You reading the plot is not part of it,' she said, mysteriously.

Then, her clothes half-ripped off her, and covered in sweat and semen, she said the words that, at that moment, I had least expected her to say.

'You haven't fooled me for a second. Do you really think that I haven't guessed who you're *really* interested in? I'm just your way in, aren't I? To finding out more about her. So you want inside information? Let me give it to you. Justine's favourite colour? Green. Justine's favourite book? *The Portrait of a Lady*. I can give you all the clues that you want. But let's cut out the crap. I haven't got all the time in the world, you know.'

TWENTY-THREE

I looked at her, wondering if it was worthwhile bothering to conceal my shock and dismay that she had discovered the truth. Had she known the truth *all along*? My plot was being rewritten by *her* and I didn't like it one bit.

Juliette seemed disinterested in my response. She also seemed indifferent to the fact that she was now writing the story.

'Of course, you are making a dreadful mistake,' she said, 'I mean with regards to Justine. She's dangerous. She is cold. She is without emotion. I may be neurotic, but at least the only person I hurt is myself.'

I watched her face as she spoke. Standing in the junk-yard of her home, as the night grew closer, the fair hair that fell in tendrils about her face turned black in the shadows. The eyes set far apart in the face were opaque. I decided to try to get back in control of the events.

'What makes you think it is Justine, not you, whom I want?'

'The disappointment in your eyes in the National Gallery when I told you I wasn't Justine – it has never left your face.'

I gave up then any thought of continuing my pretence.

Juliette started to cry. Through her tears she began to speak quietly, so that I could only just make out her words.

'She does *everything* better than I do. She also writes but unlike me she has been published. Her first novel, *Death is a Woman*, was an international success. Critics adored her literary pretensions, the public her realistic insight into character. I can't even get an agent.'

She stopped for breath and then began to speak more loudly as anger took over from pain.

'She even makes *love* better than I do. In spite of her *sangfroid*, Justine is unutterably generous with her flesh and all its hollows. Her lovemaking weaves a web: it catches her lover, like a fly, between its intricate lines. You see, I know all the intimate details. Would you like to hear how?'

I didn't know what to say. By this time her face had hardened so much, it looked as if her blood had frozen into ice.

'The only man I have ever loved told me. "*It's the way*

that she kisses me," he began. As if he were cutting off the head of a flower for his button-hole. As if the explicit details he then gave me of their lovemaking were a justification for him leaving me. Hard to believe that someone could be so cruel, isn't it? But then he *is* an artist.'

She's talking about Jack, I thought. The name on one of the corners of the square.

'She is so devious. You have no idea how. She asked for *permission* to steal him from me. That was her way. At the time her novel and Jack were only ideas in her head. She took me aside: "I want to make the hero of *Death is a Woman* an artist. Could I borrow Jack for a few days? Just for research?" I felt as if the flesh on my body would fall away as she spoke. Because I knew she was asking for the reality of him, the reality of his body and soul, not for a character in her book but for herself. There was nothing I could do to stop it from happening. How could I argue against the reality of Jack?'

The more Juliette told me about Justine, the more bewitched I became by Justine's cool treachery of her sister. Any adjective used to describe Justine, any verb to sketch in the way she behaved, only added to my desire for her. Every word to do with her had this effect on me, *no matter what the word meant*.

It had grown so dark in the room I could barely make out Juliette's outline. We were still standing in the same place where we had fucked an hour earlier. Rain was beginning to patter hard against the window pane and the skylight above. The room took on the appearance, in the increasing shadows, of a cubist painting, rectangles and circles projecting into the darkness.

TWENTY-FOUR

It was as if, once she had started, Juliette could not stop talking about Justine. Her hatred of her sister had become an obsession.

'As children, Justine and I spoke the same language. But over the years the differences have built up like bricks to form a high wall between us. It is a wall I feel protected by now. Justine knows this too: we need our differences.'

The intensity of her feelings was now finding full expression in her voice, seeping through from thought into articulation, like blood into a bandage. Even the structure of her face seemed to be concaving under the power of her emotion. The acidity of her passion was dissolving the edge of her physical features.

I was beginning to realize that Juliette might prove an unpredictable go-between for myself and Justine. But if she were still prepared to be used, I was still prepared to use her. I conjectured that the only way she had of separating herself off from her twin, was to relentlessly perceive herself as the failure and Justine as the success. The two sisters were like shadow and light. Each needed the negation of the other. Her determined reading that I preferred Justine to herself did not precipitate it as a fact (for it would have been true, whatever she did), but rather confirmed a need of her own. She had wanted me to choose her sister over her, all along. She was fed up with the gruesome shades of half-truths and betrayals that had, up until now, marked out her life. The junk in her room consisted of the trophies of all the hurts and deceptions that had filled up her mind.

Juliette had told me her story and I wanted to get on with my own again.

'Do you think you might be able to arrange a meeting for me with Justine?'

Juliette didn't flinch.

'She likes her anonymity. It is difficult for even me to get in contact with her. She is also extremely wary of strangers. She has particularly obsessive fans.'

I felt as if bars were enclosing me one by one, that any fact now about Justine, good or bad, would be made of iron. I could tell Juliette had no intention of giving me any more details tonight. I would wait until she fell asleep, and see what I could find out about Justine, on my own.

TWENTY-FIVE

I watched Juliette fall asleep, from nervous and sexual exhaustion, on the floor between a three-legged cane chair and a bag of golf clubs. In the dark she looked like just another mannequin. I wondered where to begin looking. The sheer multiplicity of objects in the room seemed to mock me, as if daring me to examine each miscellaneous object in turn, for the rest of my life. I was also reluctant to turn the light on in case I woke her.

I decided to try another room first. Coming out into the corridor, a line of doors on either side faced me, as in *Alice in Wonderland*. The first door I tried was locked, but the second opened slightly and then stuck. Shouldering the door, I shoved hard and the door opened to the sound of books crashing to the floor. A bookshelf had been propped up against the door. Inside manuscripts and books covered the floor and a single bed stood in the corner. A stuffed raven, its feathers oiled black, was perched on the mantelpiece, next to a half-full coffee cup. This was Juliette's bedroom.

I tried the tall-boy first – the drawers were filled with pastel, silk lingerie, clothing I would never have associated with Juliette. It was late and I felt tired and hadn't eaten for hours. I was also beginning to feel inexplicably nervous as I searched through Juliette's things, as if I were on the edge of some kind of disaster. A disaster that my search would directly instigate. This did not stop me looking, only made me the more determined to find something quickly, that would have to disturb me.

When I did find what I was looking for, I almost passed it by. Having unearthed a child's scrapbook from beneath a layer of frothy *negligée*, I unthinkingly flung it on to the ground. Only when the book fell face up, and open, did it catch my attention. It was a catalogue of photographs, stuck neatly in columns on to the coloured pages. Each photograph depicted an explicit sex scene between two lovers, obviously taken without their knowledge. Through each photograph a knife had been drawn in red ink on to the Polaroid snap that dissected their bodies in half. The words 'Jack and Justine' had been printed clearly above each photograph. I noticed that Justine had moles in the star shape of the plough across her torso.

'What do you think you are doing?' Juliette's voice sounded cold behind me.

Luckily, as my back was turned to her, my body was blocking her view of what I was looking at. I slipped the scrapbook under the bed and turned round. She looked terrible – rings, like huge bruises, hung under her eyes.

'I'm looking for clues.'

'Clues to where you might find Justine?' She laughed mockingly, 'You won't find them in this room. They're all up here.' And she tapped her head.

TWENTY-SIX

It was almost midnight but Juliette knew of a café under the arches which would still be open. It was still raining and to me the black stone of the bridges seemed like the entrance to the end of the world.

We sat opposite each other at a formica table eating disgustingly cooked food but I was too hungry and tired to be affronted by the squalor of the place.

'Let's get this straight,' Juliette said, her dress falling off her shoulders to reveal her scratched skin beneath. 'I *hate* Justine. I want my revenge. This is where you come in.'

'Me?'

'You. You didn't really fall for my little girl routine, did you? All that nervousness, those tears and tantrums. From the moment I first met you I have just been testing the ground to see where you stood. To find out what kind of a man you were.'

'Are you telling me that you *arranged* to bump into me at the gallery?'

'Don't be stupid. How on earth would I know that you would be there? No, *that* was total coincidence.' She smiled. 'But when I realized that you knew Justine, and even better seemed obsessed by her, it all seemed just too good to be true. I simply seized the opportunity, as any other sensible girl would have done.'

This was all getting too complicated for me. I watched

her take another sip of her tea, and desperately tried to keep up with her.

'What strikes me is the symmetry,' she said, 'You and me. Justine and Jack. Me and Jack. You and Justine. Our desires are very specific. Like those little plastic puzzles made up of letters that can only fit together in one way to form the right word. We are each one of the letters and there is only one way we can be put together to make up the word. You may have thought you were seducing me to get Justine. But I was also seducing you to get Jack.'

I looked at her, speechless. After all, she was sitting opposite me in the bright yellow light of the tiny plastic café, complacently rewriting my history. Telling me the story that I had been in was not mine, but hers all along. The story I was now finding myself in was one of obsession, jealousy and revenge but it was Juliette's.

'What do you want me to do?' I asked.

'I want you to seduce Justine.'

'*Want* me to?'

'You're being very slow.'

'You want me to seduce Justine, in order that you can get Jack back?'

'Exactly.'

'What makes you so sure that it will split them up?'

'Because Jack is a literalist. He believes in the truth.'

'What makes you so sure that Jack will go back to you?'

She laughed. '*Because, after Justine, I am always the next best thing.*'

'Where does all your faith in me come from? I might not succeed in seducing Justine?'

46

'You may think you are clinging on to some vestiges of self-control. But they have, in reality, long since gone. You are way past the point of no return. You'll get her. Whatever it takes you. It's in your eyes.'

I remained silent. I didn't tell her the extent to which my self-control was inviolable, whatever passion scratched its surface. My sense of distance from the world was profound.

However, the contradictions were proving impossible to resist.

'But why did you go through the scenario of warning me *against* Justine? Telling me about her coldness. Why did you try and put me off her, if this is what you wanted all along?'

She looked at me almost contemptuously.

'When have you ever known a man to be put off a beautiful woman whom he desires, when you tell him that she is also cold and dangerous?'

An old woman, a crone like one of the witches from *Macbeth*, bent down to collect our plates – her fingernails were filthy and she smelt of bacon.

'You don't have to trust me,' Juliette said. 'That's not necessary. Just do everything I say and everything will be all right. Justine will be yours. Look upon her as a gift. From me to you.'

Juliette had ceased completely to play the forlorn neurotic. She was now playing the part, in spite of her incongruous dress, of my business partner. With steady and appraising eyes she had just offered me a bribe. But her eyes still glittered dangerously.

Juliette's character now had been lain down by Jack.

He was responsible for the way she was, the lack of coherence to her personality, the way she was playing games with her identity. Juliette had guessed the truth about me so easily because she had become accustomed to betrayal. I was simply doing what Jack had already done to her – abandon her for Justine. Except this time I was to do it with her help. I felt as if I were following in Jack's footsteps. That whatever happened to Jack would happen to me. So my feelings about him were complex. Surprisingly, I felt no jealousy of him. He had kissed Justine in places I could only dream about. But if he were my precursor, I would be doing the same soon, too.

TWENTY-SEVEN

It was now almost one and the old woman brought us another two cups of tea which was the colour of rust and too hot.

'I'll arrange a meeting between you and Justine. But it will have to appear accidental. Justine, of course, must have no idea what is going on. After that it is up to you. I am not going to give you background material on her to help you. That isn't the way. It will sound false. She's too clever for that.'

I wondered how long Juliette had waited for someone like me to come along.

'What I said about Justine being secretive was true. She doesn't like anyone, including me, to know where she is at any given time. But she does go to one place regularly. In order to write. It is a private library in St. James's Square called the London Library. You might have heard of it. People are always putting it into their novels.'

It was early morning before I got back home to Kensington Gardens. I was relieved to return to the aesthetic sanity of my rooms. Deeds that took place in elegant surroundings somehow seemed less morally accountable. The atmosphere of Juliette's flat and the café had given a shabby air to the enterprise. After taking a bath, I lighted candles and reverently placed them on the mantelpiece below the portrait of Justine.

I felt violated by the act of sex that had taken place in Juliette's flat. That Juliette had been using her body as a means to an end made the whole encounter seem even more obscene. I lay down on the sofa and fell asleep in front of the painting.

That night I dreamt again that I am driving along the avenue of trees. I am experiencing exactly the same sensations as I have had in the previous dream, feeling the same breeze and the same sunshine on my face. But this time my sense of exhilaration begins to be replaced by a feeling of menace as I approach the house. The maze is still to the right of the house. The dream doesn't stop where it did before. I switch off the engine of the car and begin walking towards the steps of the main entrance. Then a window high up in the house catches my eye as suddenly the rays of the sun hit the glass. I cannot tell if the window is barred or whether the shafts of reflected light shine the illusion of bars across it. Someone is watching me from behind the glass. Immediately a cloud goes across the sun and the window is plunged into darkness. And I know, in the sudden realization that often takes place in dreams, that the person who is watching me from behind the window is the reason why I have come here.

I woke up the next morning, still on the sofa, my limbs aching, looking straight into the painted eyes of Justine. I leapt up from the sofa with an energy I had not felt since childhood and drew a long hot bath. This was the morning I had decided to visit the London Library.

TWENTY-EIGHT

It was London, mid-July, and the morning was hot. Heading south-east in the taxi towards the centre of town and the London Library, we had to drive through hectic and irascible traffic. A moment of doubt, a hesitation as to which direction to take, was immediately punished by horns, shaken fists and faces about to spontaneously combust. London had been heated up into a boiling mass of primeval anger. My driver was as impassive as the ferryman of Hades.

Even the pigeons were pecking each other for crumbs. Waiting in the traffic jam that encircled Trafalgar Square I watched the luminously dressed tourists splash each other in the fountains. I wondered what they made of this grotesque, enticing city. From the perspective of Nelson who was watching us all implacably from the top of his column, I was just a part of this seething mass of frantic humanity.

Inside the taxi I was suffocating, and I unwound the window for air. Trafalgar Square's sick sweet fumes of exhaust pipes swept in almost choking me. My face was wet with the heat.

'Hot, ain't it?' the taxi driver said, 'Hottest day so far. Up in the nineties, I'd say. Too hot, don't you think?'

I couldn't be bothered to reply. I watched a woman

cross the road a few cars ahead of the taxi, weaving expertly between the jam of the stationary vehicles. She was now walking down the shadowed north side of Trafalgar Square, past the National Gallery. She moved with such grace. She could have been meandering down a silent country lane in the shadows of the trees. London was only a mirage. It was when she moved into the direct sunlight and the sun caught the colour of her hair, that I saw it was Justine.

Without hesitating, I leapt out of the taxi into the cauldron of London. The voice of the taxi driver calling for his fare disappeared into the distance. I ran between the packed cars to the other side of the road, keeping my eyes at all times on her retreating back. I heard a noise, the sound of an angry engine, before I turned to my right to see the motorbike almost upon me. A dispatch rider in black leather looked straight into my eyes like the Angel of Death. We both swerved at the same time. He swerved to my right. I swerved to the left. The decision that saved my life took a split second. I watched him drive off into the distance between the gaps in the traffic jam. I turned to look for Justine but she had disappeared from sight.

I walked on to the library, in the same direction that Justine had been heading. I mused on the irrationality of my response to seeing Justine. I had *acted* as if I were completely out of control. This was out of character from my usual state of equilibrium and had nearly resulted in my death. I admitted that my thoughts may have become slightly over-preoccupied with Justine, but I had taken it for granted that I was still in control of my *behaviour*. I wanted to win her, but on my terms.

The London Library was a tall but inconspicuous building, tucked away in the corner of the square. I would not have realized it was a library but for the small brass plaque on the wall next to the wooden doors of the front entrance. On it was written THE LONDON LIBRARY and its opening times.

I walked up some steps into a large lobby. A few elderly men stood just inside the lobby discussing the painter Moreau. I walked through to the back of the main hall and climbed red carpeted stairs. Black and white photographs of distinguished male faces of famous writers peered down at me from where they hung along the staircase wall.

I opened glass doors to the reading room. A couple of members looked up from where they were sitting, as if they had just been disturbed, like birds on their nests, in the act of laying their eggs. An octogenarian was asleep under the round clock, in a large leather armchair, snoring loudly. Otherwise, apart from the hum of distant traffic, the room was silent.

I felt at home here, in a place where the intellectual prowess of a man was obviously of more value than his physical strength. Hunchbacked scholars worked here, on ancient manuscripts and first editions, as if the heat and the fevered excitement of London outside was a dream that they had just woken up from.

Justine was nowhere to be seen. I looked around the room again, but saw only the same men, sitting in the same positions, saw only the same absence. She had to be here somewhere. I had been given an omen ten minutes ago. The sighting of her wouldn't have made sense otherwise.

I became conscious of the sweat pouring down my face and I followed the staircase up to a wooden door marked GENTLEMEN. Inside I splashed my face with cold water. My face in the mirror looked like the reflection of an angel. I decided to follow the staircase up to the top floor where I found the section of the library where the books were stored. Opening another glass door, I found myself in a room where shelf upon shelf of books were running up and down the room in rows. The shelves reached almost to the ceiling. The floor was a metal grid of patterned triangles, through which I could see the floors beneath. When I looked down, I felt vertigo.

Here, it was as silent as a tomb. Not even the ubiquitous sound of London traffic could be heard. Just then, the sound of metal jangling softly started up on the floor beneath me, the sound of high heels hitting a steel grid. I looked down between the metal patterns of my floor into the room below. A woman was walking directly beneath me. A parting, straight as a knife, split the golden hair of her head in two. She was walking slowly past the shelves of books, obviously looking for one in particular. She was contained, between the two metal floors like a bird in a cage, in my moment of seeing her.

TWENTY-NINE

This time I restrained my immediate impulse, which was to call out to her. The meeting had to appear accidental. I quickly and quietly walked back along the metal floor and down the metal staircase that led down to the stored room of books below. I kept control of my breathing but there was the sound of beating wings in my head. Reaching the lower floor, I looked down the twelve tall rows of shelves but could see her nowhere. It had taken me three minutes at the most to get from one floor to the other. Surely she couldn't have disappeared in such a short time?

It was then that I saw her. She was standing at the end of the eleventh row of shelves, intently reading a book she had in her hands, her hair falling across her face. I could not understand how I had just missed seeing her. I was now only a few steps away from smelling the scent of her skin.

I pretended to be looking for a particular novel in one of the shelves. I slowly walked up the passageway of books towards her, as if in search of an author's initials that took me by chance to just beside her. Standing next to her, I took out a book at random and opened it up. I pretended to read, concentrating desperately on how I could make my first move. It was only then that I realized that I had picked out the novel *Justine* by the Marquis de Sade. The pages of the book were so thin they were almost transparent and the print from the other side showed backwards, through. My first meeting with Justine had to seem natural and coincidental.

I could smell her now. Still with my eyes focused unseeingly on the book, I decided on my plan. I would turn to Justine, nonchalantly, and ask her if she knew whether the library had a Romantic Section, or not. As a strange man asking this of a beautiful woman, the situation would, I conjectured, be ripe with comic irony. But just as I was about to look up, the words forming in my mouth, I felt a tap on my shoulder, a light tap as if a bird had just landed on me.

'I'm sorry to interrupt your reading.' Justine's hand fell from my shoulder to her side again. She showed no sign of recognizing me from the funeral. Her voice was as low and dry as the desert. 'But I need your help.'

I had to gauge my response carefully. On the one hand I had to appear surprised that a strange woman was approaching me for help in the London Library. On the other hand I had to *conceal* my surprise at the part Destiny was playing in making *Justine* approach *me*. Her making the first move gave me an advantage beyond my wildest dreams. I deliberately took a step back from her, as if almost resistant to such an out-of-the blue request, while making sure I retained an expression of helpful courtesy on my face.

Justine was even more physically perfect than I had remembered. Her eyes were as hard as precious stones set in alabaster. Her flawlessness paradoxically helped me to stay in control of the situation. It reminded me how important it was to play the part well. Her statuesque looks symbolized how high the stakes were.

'You must think it odd. Being approached by a complete stranger like this,' Justine said.

We were standing by an open window which looked out on to St. James's Square, but the air was so hot outside that it failed to alleviate the intent stuffiness of the library's interior.

'No, I don't think it's odd at all,' I lied. 'Not if you need help.'

Justine looked around us quickly but not furtively. Justine, no matter how much danger she was in, never looked furtive.

'It's difficult to speak here,' she said. She was wearing an ice-green dress of rough silk that clung closely to her body and whispered to me when she moved.

'I think I'm being watched'.

Yes, I thought, *by me*.

My reaction to her was confused, a mixture of elation that I was actually speaking to her for the first time and vague concern for the strange predicament that she seemed to be in. However, I could hardly take what she was telling me seriously – it read like something out of a bad detective novel. Part of me felt as if I were watching her act out a plot that she had taken from one of her books.

'I know it sounds ludicrous,' Justine said. 'Like something out of a bad novel.'

Just then I caught sight of a man – or was it a shadow? – dodging behind one of the rows of shelves. Justine immediately followed my line of vision but he had vanished.

'It's easy to get paranoid. The slightest twitch, sound, shadow…' She smiled at me. It was the first time that I had seen her smile. Her smile made a spontaneous connection with me, as if in the way it illuminated her face she had read what the future held in store for me. She then continued, as if unaware of the power her smile had had over me. As if unaware of the permission she had given me to share in her infallibility.

'I'd feel safer outside,' she said.

I nodded. 'But tell me first. Why me?'

'Because of your face. It is like Michelangelo's Adam reaching out to God.'

I followed Justine out of the library. She walked always slightly ahead of me as if she didn't want others to think that we were together.

THIRTY

The white heat of noon was scorching as we walked down the outside steps of the London Library. After the dark interior the bright light almost blinded me. However, Justine had the immunity of stone.

She crossed the road into the inner gardens of St. James's Square, through the black railings of the gate. The formal gardens were shaped in the form of a cross. A rose garden had been planted at its centre. Pink, gold, cream petals filled the sky, as we sat down on a stone bench within the circle of flowers. Surrounded by thorns, Justine, I imagined, could be my Sleeping Beauty. All I had to do was bend over her and wake her up with a kiss.

'He can't reach us here,' she said. I still didn't believe in the gravity of her voice. I felt as if I were just listening to her from under water.

'Who?' I asked. 'Who can't reach us here?'

Justine began to tell me her story.

'My first novel *Death is a Woman* has been published recently to huge critical acclaim. The heroine, who also narrates the story, conforms to the male stereotype of the ideal woman. The trouble is I've made her too ideal: a male fan of my writing has become utterly obsessed by her. Ironically, he has got the narrator (the heroine) muddled up with the author (me). He thinks she is me. A typical case of literary mistaken identity.

'I can hardly get touchy about a *bad reading*. The only

problem is that he's dangerous. He has written letters to me via my publisher and agent. They are obscene. But it's even worse than that – he has started to watch me, follow me around. I never catch sight of him. The only reason I know he's doing this is by the calling card he keeps on leaving me. A white ribbon. I've found them attached to trees in my garden, to the handle of my car, even my front door. What I don't understand is how he has found out where I live. I have told everyone who knows me not to let out my address to anyone.'

Her story was sounding to me more and more plausible. Regarding the fact that he had found out where she lived, my immediate conclusion was that Juliette had informed this madman of her sister's address. One way of avenging herself on Justine would be to make sure she was kidnapped by a dangerous lunatic. I would not put her hatred past anything. I was probably Plan B.

'Why don't you move? Change your identity?' I asked.

A bee landed on her dress, thinking she was a flower, and she brushed it away.

'Believe it or not, I've already tried that once. It hasn't worked. He somehow found out my new address. I'm fed up with those kinds of games. Even *I* am beginning to wonder who I am. I've also tried the police – but unless he actually causes me bodily harm they are legally unable to act. No, there has to be another way. That's where you come in.'

The seriousness of her position was finally getting through to me. I was lost in admiration for her self-possession.

'I don't want any violence, you understand. But it has

to be a stranger. I mean *you* have to be. He has been following me for months and he would immediately
recognize any of my friends if they tried to tail him.'

I stared into her invulnerable eyes. I knew that coming
to her rescue would be the only worthwhile act of my life.
Even in the full glare of the sunlight, her skin remained
pale. Even the sun was unable to touch her. Whoever this
man was, whatever kind of monster, I would track him
down.

'We will have to set a trap for him,' I said.

She nodded, 'I will ring you tomorrow.'

We said goodbye in the rose garden. She kissed me on
the cheek, but lingeringly and I realized that this was
symptomatic of her appeal – she managed to convey distance and intimacy at the same time.

I watched her walk out of sight behind the roses. Sweat
was now pouring down my body. I walked slowly
through the garden to the northern exit. It was only as I
was passing through the gate that I noticed that a white
ribbon had been tied to one of the black metal bars, hanging straight down in the still air, as if someone had drawn
a white line, with chalk, across the summer's day.

THIRTY-ONE

The passing of the next day seemed hardly bearable as I
waited for Justine to call. I dreaded to leave the flat in case
she rang. I smoked opium almost continuously in order to
dull the pain of waiting. My entire flat filled with its sweet
succulent smell, and not even the light breeze of stale
desiccated London through the wide open window could
stir its smoky haze. The days passed and still she didn't

phone. I ate nothing but fruit and dry biscuits, drinking strong Turkish coffee in order to stay in contact with some kind of reality. In the misty heat I did not bother to dress, but wandered around my flat naked, drawing a bath of cool water whenever the mood suited me.

However, even in the most depraved moments of solipsism, I still felt in control. I was *choosing* to live the days in such a manner, get through them, eradicate them from my consciousness.

The days merged in a continuum of the real, the dreamt and the hallucinated. I experienced a series of intensely erotic fantasies that involved Justine, Juliette and myself, in all combinations and positions. The visions had been so exquisite, so physically pleasurable, so corporeal, that I sometimes doubted if they had only been dreams.

But that night, when London had grown quiet outside, I started to have a vision of a different kind. A nightmarish hallucination from which I could not wake up.

As I lay reclining on the sofa, I noticed the smell first. It was the smell of excrement. Strange splashes of black paint suddenly began to appear on the wallpaper. They started to move: scores of cockroaches were scuttling over the walls in uneven lines. I leapt to my feet, only to feel my naked heels sink slowly down into a soft liqueous coldness. I looked down to see that I was standing in a morass of creamy maggots. They were crawling over the flat weave of the Persian rug in a lurid viscous slime. My palace of aestheticism had been transformed into a fetid pit.

Only when I heard the tight whirring sound of insects' wings start up did I look above me. Neon-orange moths were fluttering out of the eyes and open mouth of the portrait of Justine. On seeing this, I felt with the strong fake belief of a dream, that the real Justine had never existed. Justine was an impostor: she was just an empty shell of living insects. Justine, like her picture, wasn't real at all, she was another fabrication, another picture of death.

The phone rang. It dragged me – still panic-stricken – back into the semblance of reality. The room fell still and the hallucinations and frightened thoughts vanished into the stagnant air. I picked up the receiver: my hand was shaking.

The woman's voice on the other end spoke softly. 'Hello?' *It was her voice.*

'Justine,' I said.

'No. Juliette.' The room lurched to the side.

The sisters' voices sounded identical. I realized that I could not tell them apart. Reality wavered, shifted and took a step back.

'Juliette,' I dully repeated. I could not keep the dead weight of disappointment out of my voice.

Juliette, however, was indifferent to this. She did not take it personally. I was only her means to an end. Instead she laughed and said like a taunting schoolgirl,

'So you've tracked her down. That was quick work. But she hasn't phoned you, as she said she would? Naughty girl. I told you she liked to play games.'

I quickly told her all the details of the conversation I had had with Justine. Juliette, after all, was supposed to be on my side.

'So you think that I gave this zealot her address do you? You should be a bit cleverer than that. I may hate

her, but she is also my twin sister. I would never do anything to endanger her life. She *is* my other half.'

I remembered the photographs I had found in Juliette's
bedroom and the knives painted on to the lovers' naked
bodies and wondered if she were speaking the truth.

'Do you think that this man who is obsessed with her is
really dangerous?' I asked.

'I don't know. I do know that when someone is
obsessed they can do dangerous things. They are capable
of anything. I have read his letters and they are definitely
obscene. Unrepeatable, in fact, and I don't blush easily.
All I can say is if Justine is approaching complete strangers in the London Library *something* serious is going on.
But as far as we are concerned, it may be a blessing in dis-
guise. It will give you a chance to get to know her.' She
paused and then added, 'Don't worry. She'll phone.
Probably just when you've given up hope.'

THIRTY-TWO

After speaking to Juliette on the phone my spirits rallied
slightly. But in the bathroom I caught sight of myself in
the mirror and a stranger stared back: an unshaven man
with over-focused eyes. I quickly shaved, washed and put
on a silk shirt and jeans. By now it was late evening and
picking up a light novel I lay down on the sofa and began
to read.

A while later I had the idea of phoning Waterstone's for
a copy of *Death is a Woman*. To my surprise, at that late
hour, someone answered the phone.

'If you like, Sir, you could come on down right now
and collect it.'

I was loathe to leave the flat in case Justine phoned, but decided as it was a short journey to take the risk. I took the phone off the hook in the hope that if she did ring, on hearing the engaged tone she might try again.

Waterstone's on Kensington High Street was standing in utter darkness when the taxi dropped me off. But the anonymous face of the bookseller was waiting just inside the doors for me. I followed him into the black interior of the store. The walls were lined with books. He went over to the shelves and picked a book out and handed it over to me.

'You're lucky, Sir, this is our last copy.'

The cover of *Death is a Woman* was garish: the title was in embossed gold. A half-naked woman with a heavily made up face sat astride a chair in black stockings and gold stilettos. Her face looked uncannily like Justine's. I opened the book up. All the pages were blank. Astonished, I looked up at the bookseller for an explanation, but without saying a word he turned and walked back towards the shelves. Reaching up, he started to pull down all the books, row after row, on to the floor. They were of all categories: the Classics, Romance, Mysteries. As they fell, the books opened up their covers, like birds taking flight, revealing that they too were full of blank pages. Their shiny pale pages, devoid of print, glimmered in the shadows of the shop as they lay on the floor. The bookseller turned to face me again, his face obscured in the darkness.

'*You won't find the answers you're looking for in books,*' he said to me.

Just at that moment I was woken up by the sound of

63

the phone ringing. I had fallen asleep on the sofa. The novel I had been reading was perched precariously on my nose. I looked at my watch: it was two o'clock in the morning. I picked up the receiver, the book falling with a crash to the floor.

'It's Justine. Meet me tomorrow evening. At Nancy's Steps. London Bridge.' She hung up.

At six the following evening I was walking along the South Bank of the Thames. The cool breeze of the water took the edge off the dirty heat of the city. I wondered what kind of macabre joke Justine was playing by choosing Nancy's Steps as our *rendezvous*. It was the place where Dickens murders Nancy in *Oliver Twist*. The steps were wide and the bottom step slipped imperceptibly into the reflecting water of the river.

Justine was sitting on the penultimate step, her naked feet dangling in the water. The water distorted her pale flesh, making her feet look deformed. The large brim of a white linen hat concealed her face, as if a giant butterfly had landed on her head. Her white pinafore dress was blowing lightly in the breeze.

I climbed down the steps toward her. She looked up and saw me but instead of acknowledging me, immediately turned round again. I heard her say quietly and coolly, just under her breath.

'Sit down a few steps above me but act as if you don't know me.'

I did as she said, and looked out on to the fast flowing river which seemed potent and imperturbable. I listened.

'He's watching me now. But from a distance. He mustn't guess that we know each other. That would spoil everything. I am going to put my hat on the step beside me. Under it is a letter from him. I want you to read it.'

She did as she said, and I bent down as if to tie a shoe-lace, and slipped out the envelope from under the brim. The letter was written in clear rounded print, like a child's. Even now, with the distance of time, I cannot bring myself to reproduce the words, their meaning was so obscene. The content of the letter made it clear that he was intending to abduct her. The date that he was threa-tening to abduct her on was set at today.

'There's no one around here,' Justine said. 'Here and now is when he'll strike. This is also *our* chance to trap him. Once you've left me alone on the steps he'll make his move.'

I now knew what she was wanting me to say.

'I won't take my eyes off you,' I said. 'I'll be watching from a distance. But not far enough to let him get away.'

I watched Justine put a hand to the back of her neck. A hot summer wind blew over her, as if an invisible hand was running its fingers through her hair. Reluctantly I stood up and climbed the steps, leaving Justine where I had found her. I had no idea from which position the man was watching, but the fact that Justine and I knew about him but he didn't know about me, gave us the upper hand. There was a bench, not far away from where Justine was, on the other side of the walkway, half-obscured by a tree. Sitting on it I had a perfect view of Justine. I could even see, where the water was growing rough, the Thames beginning to splash the edge of her dress.

THIRTY-THREE

A young woman and her lover walked past me singing 'Greensleeves' in duet. An hour passed. The sun had disappeared and it was growing cold, but still I waited, Justine waited, he waited. The chill and the waiting had built up in me a numb nervous energy which I thought, if I were not careful, could verge on a sort of terror. Big Ben struck seven and the sun came out again.

An old bag lady, part of the detritus of London which kept on rising to the surface, sauntered over to me. The smell of abject poverty struck me first: she stank of urine, stale lager and cheap tobacco. What her eyes had seen had either been so terrible or so banal, it had washed all the colour out of them. She looked like one of the gargoyles from my dreams.

'Would you mind not staring at me like that?' I asked.

She laughed to reveal blood-encrusted gums where her teeth should have been. Her grey hair was long and straggly, witch's hair.

'I'm not the only one doing the staring now, am I? I imagine you've done some staring too, in your time. Not so long ago, either.' She pointed to where Justine was sitting on the steps. My view of Justine was now obscured by the tattered crone's body.

'Pretty, ain't she? Pretty as a picture. Often see her sitting there, scribbling away in a notebook. But you,' she said, 'You...' She paused and imitated how I had been observing Justine, by sticking out her neck and putting her claw-like hand under her chin. 'Just like that, you were. The Thinker.' She laughed again.

I gave her a cigarette.

'Thank you, Sir. But it doesn't do to stare like that. It makes your eyes stick out. You look quite off your trolley.'

She ambled off, leaving my view of Justine clear again. The steps were empty. Justine had disappeared. Stricken by horror and disbelief, I stood up as if the action would bring her back. *It was not possible in those few minutes*, I thought. It was not possible in those few minutes. The seconds that took place between life and death, between swerving right and swerving left.

In desperation I looked around me and saw only the couple who had been singing in duet, now almost out of sight, and the old woman disappearing round a corner in the opposite direction. Hopelessly I ran up to the steps. A stone had been placed on the penultimate step. The stone pinned down a white ribbon that was fluttering in the breeze. He had come, he had stolen her away in broad daylight, all within twenty yards of me.

White clouds scudded across the grey sky. The stone of the steps was blank, unintelligible, even tombstones have writing on them. If I could stare at the steps long enough, I could superimpose her image on to the stone, graft her back on to the present moment with the pitch of my thought. I didn't know what to do. I didn't know what to do. I wish the wind would stop blowing across my face like that, touching me like that.

THIRTY-FOUR

I began to wander down the South Bank, forlornly hoping that I might catch a glimpse of her or find a clue to her whereabouts. The abductor could have taken her anywhere, be keeping her prisoner anywhere. I dreaded to think what was going through his mind. What would he want to do to Justine but try to break her, tame her as if she were a wild horse? Judging by his letter to her his obsession was sexually out of control. He was living in his own private world where the heroine of a woman's novel had become the lynchpin of his reality.

The police station at Charing Cross was a modern building, concrete and square with brightly lit windows, but no one visible at them. It was as if the building were empty except for the concept of the law that it represented. This was the first time I had visited a police station and when I walked up the steps and entered, I was surprised by the silence, the inactivity, as if the machinery that operated the station was in another place altogether. Directly in front of the entrance was a white formica desk that ran across the length of the room. A solitary uniformed policeman stood behind it. Everywhere I looked was clear-cut and streamlined of complication. I should have foreseen then that they would have wanted a description of Justine, a form of her identity which I could not provide. I should have walked out again when I saw the artless white walls.

The policeman was looking down at his large open ledger. He had soft features, features that could be moulded only by him. It was only when I was standing in front of him, telling him that I wanted to report a missing woman, that he looked up. His eyes were dark liquid.

He printed out in his ledger her name carefully, in strong heavy lettering. I knew that, without appearing to, he had mentally registered my height, the colour of my eyes, my distinguishing features.

'How long has she been missing?' he asked.

'About an hour.'

His lips twitched slightly, to one side, as if an invisible string attached to his mouth had been pulled. I had given him the wrong answer.

'We normally wait twenty-four hours before reporting a person missing, Sir. She could have just popped out to the shops.'

Normally, I thought, yes in a normal world that would normally make common sense.

'But she's been kidnapped. He left a white ribbon behind,' I said, desperately.

It was beginning to sound like the *Scarlet Pimpernel*. I could hardly bear to meet his ironic, appraising eyes. It would be impossible to convince him of my story. Its characters were in a plot verging on the ludicrous: twin sisters, the mysterious Jack, a phantom abductor and me in a starring role. What made *the portrayal of my character* so realistic that he should have to believe in me?

'Forget it,' I said. 'It's too complicated. You wouldn't understand.'

I walked back out into the evening. But I knew it was more than just a story, I hadn't made it all up. There were the other characters in the plot to confirm it.

There was a phone box on the other side of the road. Inside, it smelt of urine. An empty crumpled white McDonald's bag lay in the corner. Cards in primary colours were stuck to the walls, advertising prostitutes. The black silhouettes of cartoon-like images of women were printed on to them. One of the glass panes was smashed, just to the right of my neck, letting the wind blow through. I dialled Juliette's phone number, trying to breathe more calmly. There was no reply. I let it ring and ring until a robotic voice told me that there was no reply to my call. I heard the chink of the returned money as I put back the receiver.

I better go home, I thought. I needed to relax – things were getting out of hand. I needed space in which to recollect myself, pull myself together. My flat would offer relief from the squalor of what was happening to me. I hailed a taxi back to Kensington. But having arrived home I could not relax. I found myself immediately dialling Juliette's number again. Still, there was no reply.

I wondered in a moment of despair if the last few weeks had only been a dream, an invention of my own making. The last month had proceeded so quickly, so intensely, I thought that if I could just eradicate it from my memory, my life would return to the tranquil solitude that I had once enjoyed. I had no proof of anything, no proof that Justine even existed, nor for that matter Juliette. Yet just because I had no proof, didn't mean I could dismiss my memories altogether. Now that Justine existed simply in my head made the burden of her image only heavier to bear.

THIRTY-FIVE

The painting of Justine that hung in my room was no longer enough. I wanted to paint a picture of her in my head with her lifeblood. The living Justine grew pale and empty with dry sockets and collapsing skin. Vampiric, the new image of her in my head sucked out her lifeblood in order to live afresh in my mind. In my head she became immortal. This fresh icon took on a life of its own, taunted me, bewitched me until I became its slave.

I started by drawing the letter J over the pages of the novel I was reading, then engraving it on the lid of my Queen Anne walnut desk. But I soon ran out of space and began on the walls, little J's, then larger, in black ink, like they were insects. J is an ambiguous letter, neither linear nor totally curvaceous. I couldn't turn it into a shape or pattern, I couldn't organize it, I just had to draw it repeatedly, over and over again. The letter was a hieroglyph: it stood for her. It was a straight line but it was also hooked. But then as I stared at the sequences of J's that lined my walls, the letter became meaningless, unreal, standing for an occult knowledge that would always be forbidden me. It stopped being the symbol for her. It stopped being the symbol for anything.

Even though the painting now failed to satisfy me as a whole, portions of the portrait still gratified me. I began to focus particularly on one area of it: the neck. It was long and white like the neck of a swan. I wanted to caress it. But her painted neck also invoked a kind of terror in me. The slim structure made me feel breakable and assailable. The neck, in spite of its chalky intransigence, reminded me of death.

The intensity of my fantasizing gradually became replaced by a realization that the real Justine had gone. I might never see her again. An atmosphere of horror filled the house, smelling of tar. I could hardly move, talk or think. My body and hands constantly trembled and when I attempted to eat my throat retched up the food, as if I had committed an act of impurity.

When I walked from room to room in my flat, my body felt distant, the deformity of my foot, however, grown to monstrous proportions.

Anger replaced fear. An anger that Justine had abandoned me. My murderous thoughts put my fingers around her throat. I was left in my hands with a wondrous creation of earth and broken bones.

However, in bed at night, the thought of her white bare body quickened my mind and my skin.

THIRTY-SIX

I began to wander around the centre of London in the vague hope that I might catch sight of her. I took buses instead of taxis, tolerating their noise and crowded smells. Their slower pace allowed me more time to survey the streets, and sitting on the top deck I had a panoramic view of the areas I had to cover. Beyond the glass, London seemed oblivious and alien. I was frightened to look at London in too much detail. I was reluctant to see its reality. I was scared that the external fact of London would split me in two.

I knew that in order to find Justine I would have to become more intimate with London's underworld. Since I had met her, it was as if London had thrown off its opera houses and art galleries, its vestiges of civilization, like a discarded cloak. No longer did I see London sheathed as the centre of cultural and political greatness. I saw the capital uncovered as a heterogeneous collection of tiny occult communities, any of which could be hiding Justine within its depths. I then had to peel back London's skin of dirt and violence and pluck out Justine from its heart.

One night I was travelling back to Kensington on a night bus, exhausted from a whole day of searching. Hypnotized by the glow of the lights in Kensington Park, I realized that their brightness only served to show up the blackness behind them. For just one moment, I took a step outside my desire, looked at my love as I looked at the park's lights from the top deck of a bus, and saw the darkness behind it. My love for Justine was reduced to a piece of luminously wrought-out fiction. My obsession was supported by the black space of unreality. I knew, looking into the shadows of the park, that only an act of blind faith could carry me through.

I gave up travelling by bus, and started to walk. I spent days exploring London on foot, stopping in transport cafés for lunch and checking into squalid bed and breakfasts at night in the hope that I might find her. Only then did I really perceive the cruelty of London. I had resisted its streetwise imperative, and because I refused to give in to its mean streets, to see them, to believe in them, London rejected me unconditionally. London left me out in the cold. But this suited me, London made a fine burial ground.

At night the cold nibbled at my skin as I wandered through the lights of Soho. The icy wind was slowly pulling the skin off my bones in strands with its thin lips. The car headlights which flashed past loud and fast, were wet and shiny with violence. The black skyscrapers veered up into the skies like monoliths to an urban god. A god that had long since abandoned his city, leaving behind the shell of his shrines. London, at night, was silent, it didn't utter words, just emanated moods of brutal unpredictability.

One evening after weeks of searching, it began to rain

and I entered a café in Charing Cross Road, to watch from the neon-lit window for a glimpse of Justine. No matter how far I travelled out to the outskirts of the city, I always returned to its centre in the end. It was a light late summer rain, and I waited for London finally to take pity on me and bring her into the café, when her defences were down, because it was raining.

THIRTY-SEVEN

It was then that I saw Justine walk past the window of the café. I ran out into the wet street, peering through the affronted crowds around me. She was walking about a hundred yards down the street, her green dress and gold hair conspicuous amongst the greyness of other women. She was moving slowly and I caught up with her quickly, tapping her shoulder as she had once tapped mine.

A face turned to look at me of horrific disfigurement. The skin had been so badly burned that any structure to the face was unrecognizable. The eyes were foamy white cataracts. The skin was a lurid red mass of scarred tissue. I quickly turned away, murmuring my apologies, whispering a case of mistaken identity. But as I walked away I felt secretly pleased at the strange woman's injury. It was her punishment for not being Justine, for making me think that she was.

THIRTY-EIGHT

I returned to my flat. The portrait of Justine had changed yet again. She was now wearing a velvet dress in the green the grass goes after it has rained. Her face was paler than usual, but full of grace, and her eyes, because they were lowered on the book she was writing, seemed shut in death. I refrained from calling out her name. It was her seeing me that would wrest all power from me. Visually, she was mine. As long as she didn't look up and see me, I had the upper hand. I was in control. I wanted to watch her forever, never disturb her, leave her trapped in her world of words so that I could just look.

My eyes were drawn irretrievably to her neck: a chain of gold in heavy loops now hung around it. It was definitely a *chain* – there was even a padlock fastened to its side. My eyes fell to her wrists, where again the same chains of gold were fastened. I could see that they weighed her down, slightly deformed the grace of her movements, as she lifted her hand to turn a page of her book. The chains were of heavy old gold, the gold of blood. The links pressed into her flesh, leaving their imprint. Only when she sat completely still could she maintain the illusion of being free.

I picked up the phone and tried calling Juliette. There was no reply. I looked at my watch – it was nine o'clock – still not too late. I decided to go round to Juliette's flat.

It had stopped raining and the August evening was humid and still. There was a light on, in her flat above the pet shop and I rang the doorbell. No one came down. I pushed against the door, and to my surprise it opened easily – it had not been shut properly. I walked through the gloomy, strangely lighted, pet shop, past the sleeping animals. In the distance I could hear the record, 'These Foolish Things', being played. As I walked up the steep steps to Juliette's flat I began to be able to make out the words: ... *and candlelight on little corner tables*. The music was coming from her apartment, the melody winding its way down the stairs towards me.

The winds of March
That make my heart a dancer
A telephone that rings
But who's to answer
O how the ghost of you clings

I knocked on the half-open door but there was no reply and I entered her flat. I walked to the end of the corridor and opened the door. The light was on. The room had been completely cleared out. It was empty except for the duck-egg blue carpet that the removal of all the junk had revealed. An empty orange juice carton stood in the corner.

I ran to her bedroom. Empty, even the bed had gone. Only a record player stood in the corner. I watched as the song came to an end, the arm of the record-player swung back to the beginning of the record and began to play the tune all over again.

A tinkling piano
In the next apartment
Somehow told me
What my heart meant
O how the ghost of you clings
These foolish things
Remind me of you …

I lay down on the wooden floor of her bedroom, my head next to the record player, letting the song interminably repeat itself, close to my ears until I finally fell asleep.

The next morning I woke up with a bad headache. The record had stuck in the groove of *lipstick traces*, playing the phrase over and over again. I switched it off. The ensuing silence returned a sense of peace to the flat. Morning sunlight was shining through the rooms. I had given up finding any clues to what had happened to Juliette. I decided that I needed some air and went to the window to open it. Jammed in the window frame was a pamphlet for Kew Gardens. I eased the folded paper out and put it in my pocket.

Closing the door to Juliette's flat behind me I went downstairs. Inside the pet shop was the musty smell of animal scent and sawdust. I stood for a moment in the shadowy light of the hypnotic blue gleam of the fish tanks. The owner was at the far end of the shop, at the front, his back to me, feeding a tank of fish. The black skin of his bared arm looked blue in the light. The Angel Fish floated slowly up towards the half-moons of his nails.

'Excuse me,' I said.

He looked round.

'I wonder if you could tell me what has happened to the girl that lives in the flat above you?'

He continued to look at me.

'To Juliette. The girl who lives above you.'

'No one lives there,' he said.

I heard a clicking sound start up. I turned round to see a hamster going round and round in its tiny red plastic wheel.

'No, I know no one lives there *now*,' I said impatiently. 'But the girl who *used* to live there. As far as I know until a week or so ago.'

'No one used to live there, neither,' he said. 'Those rooms aren't even used for storage. They're kept empty except for a couple of cardboard boxes. That's how it is. This girl you're looking for – Juliette. She's been having you on.' He smiled at me, a big smile.

I remembered her flat when I had first visited it, full of objects which had looked like the accumulation of years of habitation: the clothes, the furniture, the manuscripts. And I looked at this man's implacable face. I turned and walked out of the shop. As the door swung shut behind me, the parrot let out a piercing peal of laughter.

THIRTY-NINE

As I walked back into the centre of town that morning, various questions kept on going round and round in my head. Why had Juliette disappeared? Where had she gone? Was she, after all, in some way responsible for her sister's abduction? I remembered how she had looked when she had spoken of how she had been betrayed by Justine and Jack. The look in her eye had spiralled in on itself. Had that only been an act, to draw me in, as she had later led me to believe? What about the explicit photographs? The knives drawn through them?

Now that Juliette had gone, the only remaining character left on the plot's square was Jack. The only thing that I knew about him was that he was an artist. I also had an approximate image of his face from the photographs I had seen in Juliette's scrapbook. As I was walking, my mind hopelessly churning, my hand felt in my pocket a piece of hard card that I didn't recognize. Curious, I pulled it out – it was the Kew Gardens pamphlet that I had found in Juliette's flat. Absentmindedly, I began to flick through the pages.

Inside, was a brief history of the gardens and a list of the famous botanists who had been involved in their creation. I closed the pamphlet and was about to throw it away when the cover caught my eye. A bright colour photograph of one of the large conservatories was featured on the front, just above the times and admission prices of the gardens. A figure of a man was standing to the right, in front of the conservatory, just inside the right-hand corner of the square of the photograph. He looked as if he had wandered into the photograph by accident and was looking questioningly at whoever was taking the photograph. He did not look like a man who wanted to be trapped in Technicolour.

His face looked blunt in the outside light, the cheekbones sharp, the mouth wide and cheeky. His expression was one of making perpetual mischief. His curly hair seemed too soft and feminine for the masculine impertinence of his face. His eyes were slightly slanting in a bemused expression under the tendrils. I kept on looking at the face, beguiled by it. It was as if I had to stare at the shape of the face for a long time, in order that I might recognize it as Jack's. His body looked as if it had been draped around him for his own pleasure.

I hailed a taxi to Kew. Having paid my entrance fee, I walked through the gates, surrounded on both sides by high stone walls, into the gardens. Just inside, a long queue of adults and children were waiting for entry to the maze. I wondered why people were willing to *pay* to get lost, when they already were, for free. Perhaps they just wanted to confirm something that they already knew. It was noon and the sun was high up in the sky.

79

A uniformed warden was walking towards me.

'Excuse me.'

He looked up at me. I brandished the cover of the pamphlet and pointed to Jack.

'Could you tell me where I might find this man?'

The warden looked down at the cover and gave a smile of recognition.

'He got into there by mistake. Yes. That's John Baptiste. He works here. You'll find him over there.' He pointed just north of me to the conservatory that was also featured on the front of the pamphlet.

As I approached the conservatory, I saw a small figure running towards me down the path. As it grew nearer, I could see that she was a young girl of about nine, in a lemon dress, with long chestnut hair. Tears were disfiguring her face. She stopped when she reached me.

'I've lost my doll', she said with abrupt impertinence. 'You haven't seen her, have you?'

'I'm afraid I haven't', I replied. 'But I know the feeling.'

She looked at me crossly and ran on.

Inside the greenhouse, the air was humid – I felt it was trying to pull me inside out. I could hardly breathe. From high up above, water trickled down from carefully positioned fountains, running down the tips of the tall jungle plants, but dissolving in the heat below. I was surrounded by a dark green lushness, except for the neon flashes of orange, yellow and red blooms. The sun beat down from the glass above.

FORTY

'Can I help you?' one of the tops of the plants seemed to

ask. I looked up into the centre of the white heat of the sun. A face was peering at me from the balcony that ran along the top of the conservatory. A hand was resting on the balustrade and I thought for a moment the fingers were bleeding badly, until I saw that they were grasping a scarlet petalled plant.

'Are you John Baptiste?' I asked.

He moved out of the direct sunlight into the shade where I could see him more clearly. He was.

'Come on up. If you follow the path where you are standing, round, it will take you to the foot of a spiral staircase.'

I expected the air to grow hotter as I climbed but the fountains of water were freshening the atmosphere of the upper half of the greenhouse. Jack was bending down over a flowerpot, his back to me, planting the flower that I had seen in his hand. His fingers confidently manipulated the soil around its roots. He stood up when he heard me coming and turned to face me. He stood at least a foot above me, emanating masculine health.

'What can I do for you?'

'It's about Justine,' I said.

'It's always about Justine. You're a friend of hers?'

'She came to me for help,' I started to explain.

'*She came to you for help?*' Jack repeated, obviously astonished. 'Justine never needs *help*...'

She must have kept the threatening letters a secret from him, I thought, she didn't want to worry him.

'But surely you've noticed that she's *gone*?' I persevered.

The conversation was verging on the surreal.

'Oh, I never worry about that. Justine is *always* disappearing. She's *addicted* to disappearing. She does it to make her life more interesting – to compensate.'

The heat of the greenhouse was making the headache that I had had since I had woken up, worse.

'Compensate for what?' I asked.

'For not succeeding as a writer.'

'But she's a successful writer!'

'Who on earth told you that?'

'Both Juliette and Justine.'

'Oh, they're as bad as each other.'

'Are you saying that Justine has *never* been published?'

'Never. She has been working on a novel called *Death is a Woman* for years, but she can't get the plot to work out. Or the characters, for that matter: they all seem to merge into each other. So she lives her *life* as if it were a novel instead. It livens things up for her – she's the prototype drama queen. Don't worry that she has disappeared. In fact, now that you mention it, I remember her telling me she was leaving the house for a few days.'

'When was this?'

'About twelve days ago, I think.'

Twelve days ago was the day that she had been abducted. This was making no sense. Had Justine *known* that the abductor was going to be successful? Ridiculous. For whatever reason, Jack was lying.

FORTY-ONE

I realized that there was no point in my explaining to Jack the true circumstances of Justine's disappearance. I took his phone number and his address and left realizing that he knew even less than I did. And also feeling, since our meeting, that I now knew less than I had done before. The more I thought about it, the more convinced I became that Jack had been lying. If *Death is a Woman* had not been published, how could the abductor have become obsessed by its heroine? The only person who had read her writing was Jack. Surely he couldn't be the abductor? But if he had followed Justine for all those weeks, wouldn't she at some point have caught a glimpse of him and recognized him?

I climbed back down the spiral staircase, through the artificial rain. A few minutes later I heard the sound of running footsteps and my name being called. I turned around to see that it was Jack.

'Do you mind if I walk with you a while?' he asked. The light changed the colour of his eyes from slate grey to blue.

We walked down towards the lake. He's like Puck, I thought, a grown-up Puck. He causes trouble. Wherever he is, his sense of playful irresponsibility, his lack of intro-spection, will cause trouble. He will be the catalyst for his own destruction. He will be the carrier of distorted mes-sages. This is the man whom Justine loves.

'Do you love Justine?' I suddenly felt compelled to ask.

'Love is …' he paused and then laughed. 'Love is … like an armchair cover. It hides a multitude of sins. It's washable and may well have a riot of roses and auriculas splashed over it, but underneath everything is all ripped up.'

He turned and looked directly into my eyes. His eyes were now blue black like the water of the lake. A child's pram was floating in the water.

'Do *you* love Justine?' he asked.

I was taken aback. It had not occurred to me that he would attempt to analyse my feelings, that he had a consciousness of his own that would not be acting in exact conjunction with my own.

'How can you ask that, if you don't, as you have just implied, believe in love?'

'Ah, but you do and so does Justine. So why don't the both of you play let's-pretend?'

He skipped a stone across the surface of the lake. It bounced six times.

Something plastic squashed beneath the heavy platform of my right foot. I had stood on a doll. I bent down and picked her up; she was in a hot pink dress, with frothy golden curls and forget-me-not eyes. She batted her eyelashes at me.

'You should hand her in,' Jack said before turning away and walking back towards the greenhouse.

I put the doll under my jacket, obscurely angry with the little girl who had lost it for being so careless. Arriving home, I phoned Waterstone's but there was no reply. I stuck the doll up on the mantelpiece, just under the portrait of Justine. She had been lost, and I had found her, and I had taken her home where I could keep her forever.

FORTY-TWO

The events of the story of Justine had become my new drug of choice. But I saw through the haze of my obsession that blood was now dripping from one of Justine's painted eyes.

The letter arrived the next morning. It lay propped up on my mantelpiece, a missive from the underworld, defiling my sanctuary. My name and address were written in the unformed handwriting that I now immediately recognized. It did not occur to me to wonder how the abductor had found out where I lived. I opened the letter with a mixture of fear and anticipation.

The words on the page were like a visitation from the devil. All the feelings of my mind and body rose in revolt against its words. For the whole of my life I had been surrounded by a wall of beautiful artifice. Yet from the moment I had first seen Justine my protective fortification had been toppling in pieces, one by one, around me. First the wall around the fortress, then the towers of the fortress itself, stones whole and broken, falling hundreds of feet down into the waiting grass. Dust motes were hanging in the air.

I looked again at the only words that had been capitalized on the closely written page: KILL JACK OR JUSTINE DIES. The abductor's jealousy of Justine's love for Jack was stuck between the barbed-wire of his other obscenities like a black paper flower. The words were only made of black print.

I blocked out the letter from my memory. However, over the next few days London's violence seemed to intensify accordingly, become its very heartbeat. The tensions in the streets had been normalized by the words of the letter, become part of a larger pattern. Everywhere I now looked I saw the imagery of death. On television, in newspapers, in film. As if the imagery of the world had come up to meet my own private world.

FORTY-THREE

I arranged to meet Jack the following Saturday: he suggested Leicester Square. Arriving early, I was met by a seething mass of humanity which filled up the square with its noise and smells and gestures. The multicoloured lights and arching machinery of a fair had been erected in the square's centre. Ferris wheels revolved high up in the sky to a discordant cacophony of musical tunes. People of all ages and colours, their faces strained by the need to have a good time, shoved violently around me. The crowd swallowed me up before I had time to escape: they had violent whims which pushed me any which way.

Jack was heading straight through the crowd towards me. He was conspicuous as if parting the sea. He seemed to have no difficulty in walking in a straight line through the crowd, as if the crowd were moulding itself to his intentions. In spite of his broad shoulders he was walking with the still head and lithe movements of a ballet dancer. Jack seemed to be full of these supple contradictions. As if his body couldn't make up his mind about who he was, or perhaps it was because he himself didn't care. Leaning over the shoulders of the crowd, he reached out his hand to me. I took it, reluctantly: his palm was cool and dry. He dragged me gently in the direction of a building which stood to the side of the square, fronted by stone steps. Climbing the steps, we stood above and apart from the crowd.

As we stood together in silence watching the crowd, it began to gently rain. Water trickled down Jack's hair and over his face. I realized that in spite of his contradictions, there was something very specific about him: his sexuality. And as soon as I thought this, a sense of repulsion engulfed me. It repelled me to think of his body heaving over the pale ethereality of Justine.

The rain was stopping.

'All's fair in love and war,' Jack said. Before I had time to resist he had seized my hand again and was dragging me back down into the crowd.

FORTY-FOUR

The nearer the centre of the square we drew, the deeper I felt we were travelling into an underworld of lost souls. The Ferris wheel was circling high up in the sky ahead of us, a bangle of sparkling light.

Jack stopped in front of the gun ring. It was a stall with a row of fluffy teddy bears and Barbie dolls standing in shadow at the back. The woman behind the stall had the callous shrivelled face of those who work for the entertainment of others. She had sold off all her joy long ago. She handed Jack a gun. Her smile was as yellow as a plastic duck.

Jack confidently picked up the gun, held it to his shoulder and took aim at a fluffy green teddy bear. He shot it between its plastic eyes and it slowly toppled over to one side.

'Your turn,' he said, smiling and handing the gun over to me.

'I don't know how to,' I said.

Standing behind me, he placed the gun in the crook of my shoulder and altered my grip. I could feel his breath on the back of my neck.

'Aim the barrel of the gun between the two points at its tip.'

Magically, the tip of the Barbie doll's pert nose became centred in my view-finder.

'Pull the trigger. Now,' he said.

I fired and the Barbie doll fell off her perch on to the sawdust floor.

'See, it's easy when you know how,' he said.

We began desultorily circulating the fair again. All the lights of the fair were in the primary colours: blues, yellows and reds, major not minor tones. But they couldn't compete with the flesh-coloured light of London that constantly shines up in the sky, that is never shut off, that hovers over London like a halo. The fair lights are the lights of a toy lamp compared to the pervasive presence of the city light.

There are no stars in the sky of London any more. Like the fair, they couldn't compete with the city. Instead of flashing in different colours to make an impression, the stars went out. London, with a huff and a puff, blew them all down.

'You take life seriously, don't you?' Jack asked.

I was startled out of my introspection.

'I don't tell jokes, if that's what you mean,' I said.

'Not exactly. I meant that you seem to be missing a sense of irony. You're like the boiling frog.'

'The boiling frog?'

'It was a scientific experiment. If you put a frog in boiling water it jumps out again immediately. If you immerse a frog in cold water and gently heat it, it remains in the water until it boils to death. The frog just doesn't notice what's happening. That's what you're like with your seriousness. You are sitting happily immersed in your lack of irony. Not noticing that, imperceptibly, it's boiling you alive.'

We were both sitting on painted horses waiting for them to begin circling. The Kinks were playing 'You've Really Got Me' over the loudspeakers. One of the painted eyes of my horse had been scratched out. My horse was on the inside of Jack's and lagging slightly behind.

'But, I could say the same about your lack of seriousness,' I retaliated. 'You treat life as one long shaggy dog story.'

'At least being boiled to death by a running joke is more fun.'

'Only if it's a good one.'

The horses slowly started to revolve, going up and down to the music.

'But don't you see,' Jack said, 'that you can take life either way? And that either way is neither right nor wrong. If you treat life lightly or intensely it comes down to the same thing in the end. Death. So why not enjoy yourself in the meantime?'

The words 'You've got me so I can't sleep at night' blocked out the rest of his words. I watched, feeling distant, his mouth opening and shutting like a goldfish in a plastic bowl.

FORTY-FIVE

The horses were going round faster and faster. I clutched on to the pink fibre of my horse's mane which cut into my hands. London was passing me by in increasingly faster circles.

'Perhaps we're two different sides to the same coin. My frivolity and your intensity. The same selfish coin,' Jack suggested.

'That would be a turn up for the book.'

The horses were slowing down, London was coming to a standstill again. Jack's curly hair was tousled. I tried to control my envy of his *joie de vivre*. No, we were not alike. I watched the lines at the corners of his eyes wrinkle up when he smiled, laughter lines.

We walked back out of Leicester Square through the disintegrating crowds that were dwindling along Charing Cross Road. The music of the fair faintly echoed in the distance. I felt tired and oddly satisfied. It occurred to me that we had spent the day more like two lovers, than like two men who supposedly loved the same woman. We said goodbye at Trafalgar Square. Nelson's column was lit up from far above us.

I put out my hand reluctantly to shake his hand. But Jack moved his face towards mine and abruptly kissed me hard on the mouth. The stubble on his chin felt coarse. His mouth tasted of alcohol, his lips were wet, his tongue just flickered. I stepped away violently from him but he was smiling.

'Either way, it makes no difference,' he said.

He turned and walked away.

I turned back home with a deep sense of triumph. Jack's bisexuality was a weakness, a nebula. It rendered his identity inchoate. It was a secret that he had casually dropped onto the ground in front of me and which I could now pick up and nurse to the point of its suffocation.

FORTY-SIX

The floor is uneven, the narrow cavities in the rocky floor making it difficult to walk. But I can hear the faraway screams of a woman's voice. The scream is of pure thin pain. A sound where language has become irrelevant, replaced by the body's direct expression of agony. The nakedness of the sound arouses me. It pierces to the centre of my soul.

I turn the corner. Justine, naked, is chained to the black walls of rock. Her white flesh is bleeding as if someone has drawn a map of an unknown country, in red ink, on her body. The walls of the dungeon are sweating water, and I can smell the sweet stench of decaying flesh.

The abductor is bent down over her. I can make out from the movement of his back and the crack of a whiplash that he is whipping her. Justine's face, which is turned in my direction, is contorted by need and desperation, wet with tears. Her face has concaved and her eyes have disappeared into a grimace of pain. But when she sees me her face lights up. She stretches out her arms towards me in supplication.

'I've come to rescue you,' I say to her.

On hearing me speak, the abductor straightens up, lets his whip drop to his side and turns around. He looks straight into my eyes. But I am looking back into my own eyes, the abductor has my face. He looks like an angel. I step back in fear, turn, run back through the passageway hearing his footsteps running behind me, the same arhythmic limping, chasing me, knowing that if he is to catch up with me it means my death. For it is impossible that the two of us can co-exist in the same world.

FORTY-SEVEN

Over the following days the distinction between my identity and the abductor's became less and less clearly defined. I began to feel almost as if he were my alter ego. He had captured Justine, was watching her, looking after her, loving her. He was carrying out the extreme point of my desire.

The thought of making Justine my slave began to preoccupy me. She would show utter sexual devotion, perform every sexual gratification or whim. I fantasized about the malleability of her body, her shifting position, her opening-mouth, her touching-hands, her wide-open legs that revealed the rose interior of her. I would keep her chained to the bed like a dog.

It was Jack who was the true monster, not the abductor. It was Jack who was incapable of passion. Jack was indifferent to Justine, worse, flippant about her. It was Jack who was the abuser of Justine, not the abductor who, because of the power of his love for Justine, could not help himself. The abductor shared with me an overwhelming passion for Justine. Jack, however, had retained total self-control. He was not made vulnerable by the power of his obsession. He was not one of us. How could *his* cursoriness compete with the concentration of our ardour? *He* was the one that should be punished. The realization had come suddenly but had crept over me with the inevitability of the truth.

FORTY-EIGHT

As I grow older, the fragility of life becomes real for the first time. The gap between life and death narrows to a slit. The effort of my life no longer concentrates on living but on preventing my life from being arbitrarily snatched away. Life is curled up in bed like a newborn baby. At any moment a strange woman can come in and seize it, choosing that baby simply because of the way the hair curls on its forehead. But there is a way in which I can gain control over life: by controlling death. I can choose when death will visit, instead of waiting for death to choose me.

When I phoned up Jack and asked him round to Kensington Gardens, I was choosing when Death would pay a visit. Soon I would be able to hold Jack's life, as Juliette had held the starling, encircle his life with my thumb and forefinger, and be able to feel the pulsating of his heart beat against my palm.

Jack was no longer a man but a symbol. A symbol made flesh incarnate, the skin wrapped over his bones, the flesh that held his blood, the pulsing blood, all contributing to the bloodline that separated me from Justine. A symbol of the obstacle to winning her love. The superficiality of his nature, his promiscuous sensibility, were undeserving of Justine's love. Her love, which by all the rights of Destiny, belonged to me. He was nothing but a common thief. I would not be killing him because of the abductor's threat that if I didn't I would never see Justine alive again. (I did not believe in this). I would kill Jack because, like the abductor, I could not bear to see him remain alive.

FORTY-NINE

When Jack entered the drawing-room at noon, he made no comment on the portrait of Justine hanging on the wall. Under his arm he carried a painting wrapped up in brown paper so that I could not see what it represented. He handed the parcel to me. I was struck yet again by the aura of his physical well-being. He was a painter, a creator, not like me, a collector. He had not been paralysed by the definition of what was art. I carefully unwrapped the painting and leant it against the sofa.

The painting was a grotesque meaningless jumble of different lines in clashing colours. The colours were in slurry dark shades of muted browns and greys. These were muddy, earthy colours, dirty and entrenched. Gashes of vulgar orange and lime peeped through the monstrous murkiness. The painting gave off an odour of sickly intimacy, a green stench.

'You don't like it?' Jack asked. I could tell by his amused, patronizing tone, that his sense of confidence in his own talent was set as hard as concrete.

'I don't understand what it is about,' I said. I was also surprised. Hadn't Juliette told me that Jack was a literalist, a believer in the truth? How many more versions of the truth could I stand?

'So you don't think it's a good likeness?' Now I really felt that he was laughing at me.

'That's a *portrait*?' I asked, flabbergasted.

'Don't you recognize her? I was painting from a photograph.'

He handed me a photograph which he had taken from

94

his pocket. It was a Polaroid of Justine, naked, sitting in an obscene position. She had moles, in the star shape of the plough across her torso.

'Did she know that photograph was being taken?'

'Justine *loves* to have dirty photographs taken of her. Look at her – she's posing.'

I thought of the photos I had found in Juliette's flat. Was Justine somehow involved in the taking of them, rather than an innocent victim of Juliette's jealous voyeurism? But this photographic image of Justine was not of the Justine I knew. This was a different vulgar Justine, a woman who exhibited her sexuality like a whore, a Justine that I would not believe in.

Looking more closely at the painting I could begin to make out the shape of Justine's face, surfacing from the incoherence of the contradictory colours and the vehement brushwork. But her face had been deformed. Cut into blocks. And the delicacy of her drawn-back face had been smashed, turned into flabby slabs of thick oil paint. Her lucid eyes had been slit into grimaces of malicious intent. The soft wide mouth prised open into a twisted scream. All traces of her aloof serenity had been eradicated, instead this monstrous defamation of feminine beauty was all *there* intrusive, demanding and repulsive.

'There are different versions of Justine,' Jack said. 'That is mine. Who's to say which one is right? Justine's sister, Juliette, looks just like her. But whereas Justine demands nothing from me, Juliette pulled, like a child, at my soul. But who's to say that Juliette isn't just another version of Justine? The version that I hurt.'

'But what about Justine? *She* must know which version is right?'

'I care what Justine *thinks* as little as you do.'

FIFTY

Jack brought out a hammer from one of his jacket pockets.

'What's this for?' I asked.

'For hammering a nail into the wall. I thought I'd help you hang the painting.' He placed the hammer on the window sill. He then sat down cross-legged on the carpet beneath the painting and I sat down beside him. He poured me a glass of malt whisky from the bottle that he had brought. His nails had puce red paint beneath them, the exact same shade of red that Juliette had had on her cheek, the day I first met her at the National Gallery. But she had told me she had not seen Jack again since he had left her for Justine. So how *could* it be the same red? It had to be a different red.

'You remind me of myself,' Jack said, 'when I first met Justine – besotted. She was like a blank canvas on which I could paint my desires. I ended up with *that*.' He pointed to his painting of her.

I looked at the painting again. The picture was confirmation that he had to die. I had to kill him to save her image from his superficial vision. This man had turned her beauty into a misshapen monster. He, in that representation of her, had systematically mutilated, murdered her beauty. He was indifferent to the single truth of Justine. That was why his hands were bloody with red paint. He did not need, as I did, the image of her beauty to breathe.

A smile had crept over Jack's mischievous face – he had the charm of the devil. The stench of the painting was starting to emanate from its creator. I watched aghast, as his hands began to grow long and thin, the skin of his body translucent. His features started to concave before my unwilling eyes. The sides of his eyes ran down his face, dipping into the upward sardonic curve of his mouth which was rising impossibly high up the side of his face. The shadows of his features hardened into black lines as the skin grew paler. He now looked like a two-dimensional sketch of a pattern of black ink on a white page, unreadable but with its own internal logic.

At that point it became clear what I had to do. I had to return the incoherence of his face to a pattern that made sense. But just by looking, I couldn't restore the symmetry back to Jack's face. The lines shifted around, became even more unintelligible, the harder I stared. I turned round to look at the portrait of Justine for help.

Someone somewhere said my name.

From where I was sitting on the carpet I looked up at the window sill. The hammer was lying on it. The hammer was of standard design: an oak handle, dark metal. It only took a second to reach up and take it down. It seemed unnaturally light. I had the sensation that the hammer might float out of my hands unless I held onto it tightly. I clutched at the handle tightly, trying to feel it. The tool now seemed like a phantom limb. A necessary part of me that I had lost and now didn't really exist: an instrument of let's-pretend.

It was heavy enough. Jack watched me, silently, taking a sip of his whisky. He looked at me in amusement as I stood up, raising the hammer above my head. He looked as if he were about to ask me a question.

FIFTY-ONE

The first blow only knocked him unconscious. I looked down at his face as he lay on the floor. He looked vulnerable, fair, his outstretched arms flung up behind his head where he had tried to fend me off. A tenderness overcame me. My anger dissipated, seeped away, like the trickle of blood that was now seeping from the side of his head. Seeing Jack's body lying there, abandoned, I was overcome by a kind of desire – not for him but to be him, to be that sexual, that prone, that oblivious to life.

I brought the hammer down over his face again. I brought the hammer straight down on his face, splintering the nose and feeling the iron head sink into the cheekbones as if they were made of paper. It was only when the iron met bone did the weapon finally judder into existence. And I felt a surge of power, a sure sense of rightness. The handle seemed to course into my bone. Instead of it being a phantom extension of me, I became the phantom extension of it. I became as strong as its iron head, as ungiving and virulent. Blood splashed over the room, over my face and clothes and over Jack's painting of Justine, just adding another colour to the colours that were already there.

From above the mantelpiece, Justine watched the scene that was taking place in front of her, with equanimity. Her presence now promised moments of pleasure as soft as melting snow.

FIFTY-TWO

But Jack's face: instead of mending the asymmetry, I had smashed it even further, shattered his identity into pieces of bone. I had done what he, in his painting, had already done to Justine. But at least it was an asymmetry that I had created. Its design was mine. And my identity remained intact while Jack's lay in pieces on the floor.

The blood sprouted from him in spirals and pretty curls like ivy growing across the floor, where there is no sun for it to grow upwards. His flowing blood was the only sign of life or movement. The blood was spiralling across my carpet. Watching it decorate the floor in scarlet lines it suddenly occurred to me that if I wanted I could bend down and dip my finger into its stream. Before I was conscious of what I was doing the tip of my finger was hovering over the surface tension of the blood, then breaking down through it to the soft hot liquid beneath. I lifted the red-stained fingertip to my lips. The blood tasted salty, warm and meaty, the blood tasted of life.

I went into the kitchen and fetched a knife. Kneeling down beside the body, I carefully carved out the skin around the area above his heart. I wanted to find out if the heart, the temple of love, went on beating just a little while after death, if the heart, like the blood, carried on the momentum of life. I lifted up, like a heart-shaped hinged lid, the serrated flesh of Jack's chest. But there was no heart beneath. In the place where the heart should have been there was just an empty space.

FIFTY-THREE

Once I had completed my task, the physical attributes of
Jack were unrecognizable. I had had to use a saw to dis-
member the limbs and sever the head. It was unlikely that
anyone would connect me with Jack, but I had spoken to
one of the wardens at Kew Gardens, and Juliette also
might prove unreliable. I didn't want the body identified.
I put the pieces of Jack's body in a black bin liner,
together with the hammer, the knife, my bloodied clothes
and the saw. Having bathed and dressed again, I slipped
the photograph of Justine into my pocket, tied the bag up
and with difficulty hoisted it over my shoulders like a bag
of swag.

In case I was recognized, I thought it safer to go by
underground, rather than taxi or bus. I took the tube train
to Tower Hill. Overground it was a dull wan day. The
Tower of London, with its newly scrubbed beige stone,
looked like a child's cardboard toy. The Thames, beyond
the deserted building sites, was opaque and grey. The sky
moved at an identical slow heavy pace above it. I walked
down the Highway, where there were no shadows.

I crossed under a subway which was lit by a neon light,
my feet echoing down the tunnel. It was like walking
through a tomb. I was half-way through it, when a figure
appeared at the other end. At first I thought it was a
dwarf, he was walking so hunched and keeping so close to
the side of the wall. However, he straightened up as he
came towards me. He was about my height.

It was only as he passed me, that I heard a click. I
thought it was the snap of someone's fingers. I felt the

cold touch of metal pressed intimately against my neck. I put down the bag.

In spite of the apparent directness of his lavender blue eyes, I felt as if he were staring right through me, that he wasn't looking at me at all. Those eyes didn't see straight, they saw the world in disconnected shapes. They told me I was going to die. *I thought of Justine.* He put his other bony hand out and traced a pattern round my face with his fingers, a pattern that only he could understand.

However, as he drew the design on my face, a dull glimmer of recognition appeared in his gaze. Still with his flick-knife against my throat, he said,

'Haven't we met before?'

I almost wanted to laugh. I had never seen him before in my life. But he had smelt the connection, seen my affinity with death engraved in my face like initials carved in stone. He lowered the knife. Shrugging his shoulders, he continued his journey down the subway and round the corner, the sound of his footsteps receding into the distance. I put my finger to my throat and came away with a single drop of blood. I felt exhilarated, as if I had passed some kind of test.

Picking up the bag again, I walked back under the subway and took a detour out onto the barren wasteland that separated the Highway from the river. The glass and steel of the Docklands glimmered in the distance. The bag became increasingly heavy and I had to keep stopping to regain my breath. It was now 5 pm.

FIFTY-FOUR

The area was desert, the ground consisting of dry earth

and the odd piece of discarded machinery. There were no birds here, no insects, no sound, except for the ever present hum of London's traffic, like a Greek chorus. The only movement was pieces of litter and old newspapers that fluttered in the wind. The sky above was white and unforgiving. From inside the bag on my back, I could hear the dead man's thoughts whispering to me, to the hesitant rhythm of my walk.

What I thought was flat land to the river turned out to have a slight dip in it which was invisible until I was upon it. In the small ash-white valley two youths and a woman were boiling a saucepan of water on a wood fire. They had set up home here: makeshift tents and boxes and empty cans were strewn about them. Through the flickering flames of heat the river shimmered like a mirage.

The group stood up as I approached.

'What have you got there?' the young woman asked.

Her voice managed to sound intimate and insolent at the same time. She had too much space in the centre of her forehead – enough room for her cunning and stupidity.

'A dead body,' I replied.

They laughed, and, suddenly disinterested, returned to watching their fire.

Ten minutes later I had reached the edge of the river. The group of teenagers had disappeared out of sight again into the dip behind me. The water was black and glittering as if scattered with diamonds. With a last surge of energy, I hurled the bag far into its depths, and watched it gulped down. The simplicity, the order to the deed struck me.

I returned to Kensington Gardens, ecstatic but tired, and quickly bathed and changed again. I could not bear to be dirty or feel unclean: the blood-spattered flat strangely did not bother me.

Lethe lay curled in the corner, thin and neglected. I was conscious, since the murder, of moving with more grace. I put the photograph of Justine up on the mantelpiece, next to the doll and underneath the portrait. The blood on the photograph was proof that I had done what had been requested. Jack's blood represented Justine's life. I picked up the doll and turned her upside down: she made a mewing sound.

FIFTY-FIVE

During the next few days I went about my daily business, but with the uncanny feeling that I was in some way sorting out my affairs before beginning a long journey. I sorted through papers, sifted through art catalogues and went to the occasional auction at Christie's. However, all the time I was waiting for a sign.

The final night that I spent in my flat I dreamt I was driving up the avenue to the house again. The maze is still to the right as I approach the house. Someone is looking at me from the window above. I get out of the car and this time, as I approach, the door mysteriously opens. I then seem to split into two people as I watch, from a position high up in the sky, myself walk inside the house and disappear, the door shutting behind me. The Gothic house stands completely still in the sunlight. The person standing watching at the window has also gone. The scene now is devoid of humanity. I can see no one in the house and the car stands empty on the driveway. Except that I know that I am now inside the house, and another person is in there, waiting.

FIFTY-SIX

I was woken up from my dream by the sound of the phone ringing. The luminous dial of my alarm clock read 3 am. Immediately alert, I picked up the receiver.

'It's Justine. Have you done it?'

For a moment I couldn't think what she was talking about.

'Yes... Yes.'

'Have you got any proof? To show him?'

'Yes, a photograph. Of you. It's covered in his blood.'

'Thank you,' Justine said. 'I will never be able to thank you enough.' Her lack of anguish over Jack's death only seemed to point to the seriousness of her position. It made me take the abductor's threat to her life more seriously. The abductor's identity and my own separated out again.

'Does the person who's kidnapped you know that you are talking to me?'

'He's standing beside me. I'm just repeating what he says. Like a ventriloquist's doll. He wants you to come out here. As soon as possible. He wants to meet you. He thinks that you are both one of a kind.'

She gave me the address, which was out of London, in the country.

'I'll be there by tomorrow evening. Are you alright?'

The phone went dead.

I couldn't go back to sleep: I would be seeing Justine tomorrow. What to do then, how to rescue her, would depend on my wits and ingenuity. I had come this far and I had no intention of failing now.

FIFTY-SEVEN

The next morning, I realized without a shadow of a doubt that I would be leaving my flat, forever. Justine would now be enough. My flat seemed like a dead religion, a church empty of significance. The paintings, the statues, the patterned tapestries all seemed irrelevant. They were hollow artefacts, even the portrait of Justine had shrunk to a simulacrum. I was about to own the real thing. I packed a suitcase of a few clothes, and some money. Lethe looked on indifferently from the corner which she had not stirred from in days.

I kept the methylated spirit underneath the bathroom sink. I unscrewed the lid and took the bottle through to the drawing-room where I splashed the spirit over the blood-stained sofa, the carpets, the Chippendale chairs, the walls, Jack's blood-stained portrait of Justine. The strong succulent smell made me feel light-headed. I went up to the doll I had placed on the mantelpiece and soaked her dress in the inflammable liquid. I struck a match and set fire to her. The flames engulfed the doll immediately, the plastic face concaving, as if at first she were about to burst into tears, then into irreparable deformation. The photograph of Justine, propped up beside the doll, melted into streams of red and gold. The flames quickly licked upwards towards the portrait of Justine above the mantel-piece. I saw her smiling at me between the flickering flames as the paint dripped off her face.

I picked up my suitcase and made my way out of the

burning flat. I wondered how long it would be before someone called for help. What mattered was that they waited long enough for all my mementos to beauty to be destroyed. I no longer needed them. I was about to rescue and possess the icon of beauty itself. As I got into the lift of my apartment block and shut the heavy black metal gates together, I could taste the acrid smell of burning in my mouth and hear the other-worldly screams of Lethe being burned alive.

I was euphoric – by burning my flat I had eradicated my solitary past in preparation for a future with Justine full of exquisite pleasure. As I climbed into the taxi I turned my head to take one last look at my flat. Flames were beating out of the windows of my top floor, angry and impassioned, demanding gratitude for their force of will. I never doubted their power to cleanse.

FIFTY-EIGHT

Outside Kings Cross was purgatory: beggars, drug dealers and pimps. Lost souls waiting for their bodies to return to them. The bright lights of London lit up around them, like the fires of Hell. Inside the station, the light that shone through the vaulting arches belonged to God. Stations always beguiled me. They seemed to me full of containment and the largesse of the soul. They were the gateway to the other side.

As the train moved out through the suburbs, I realized that this was the first time I had travelled out of London since I had met Justine. Justine had become terminally connected with the city, it was where I thought she had been imprisoned, where I had looked for her traces.

The train was almost empty. The windows were not tinted, but muddied with dirt. The gentle murmurs of the passengers served as a fluid melody to the rhythm of the train, like a stream of blood to the beating of the heart. The train rumbled on through the dark countryside. It was misty and foggy outside. But the sky above was as white as Justine's flesh. The light was so bright that it hurt my eyes.

I was certain that light also lay in wait for me at the end of my journey. A light that would engulf any pain in the moment it took to blind me with its brightness. This light would be jealous of any pain, burn it out of existence. Only the angel of terror and pleasure would be left to hover above my head.

In the opposite compartment, twin girls were playing chess. Their profiles were identical, their movements synchronized. They could have been one person reflected in a mirror.

The train stopped at a small provincial town and an old woman got on. Much to my annoyance she sat down opposite me. Her damp grey hair fell in strands around her ears.

'Would you mind not staring? It's very rude,' she suddenly said to me. Her breath smelt of linctus.

'I'm sorry. I didn't realize that I was,' I said.

'Well, you should have. You strike me as someone who is not very observant of someone else's feelings. Or of your own, for that matter. You shouldn't go through life with so little self-awareness. It could end in trouble.'

She was quite clearly insane, and I was relieved when she got off at the next station. I watched her stride along the platform. She was smiling. In spite of her age, she looked very far from death. Further away from it than I was.

FIFTY-NINE

It was late afternoon when I arrived in the small village that Justine had told me was in the vicinity of my final destination. The place was idyllic, on the verge of unreality – the pretty cottages looking as if they were made out of pillarbox-red cardboard, and the village pond out of coloured glass. I hired a convertible and followed Justine's elaborate directions out of the village, to the stone pillars which formed the gateway to the drive. I turned up the driveway, the wind blowing across my face, the sun coming out in a last-minute appearance before nightfall. The avenue of trees cast shadows on the driveway, the leaves were just on the edge of turning gold. I had been here before.

Looking back now, as I write, I think the journey to Justine's, that day, was the happiest of my life. No other emotion can compare to the sense of freedom, laughter and erotic anticipation of meeting someone with whom one has fallen in love. The danger involved in my journey heightened my excitement. If I had my life over, I would wish simply to be approaching forever the stone gates of the driveway and driving up through the shadows of the trees, the smell of leaves and grass in my head, the sunlight full on my face, with the first and only total sensation of freedom I have ever had.

The recognition of what was happening to me now, from the dreams that I had already had, reinforced my sense of Destiny. This was where I was supposed to be. The last few months had been leading up to the inexorable fact of the present moment. The sound of the birds, the fresh breeze, had all been experienced before in my dreams, to make their happening now a form of welcome, a kind of reward.

I turned the corner of the avenue to be faced with the Gothic house of my dreams. I stopped the car and walked out across the gravel. Looking up I saw someone at the window staring down at me from between the bars. The sun lit up the glass, blinding me for a second, and then went behind a cloud. I could now see the face clearly – it was a woman's. It was Justine. Who else could it have been? There was a humming in my head as I approached the steps of the main entrance and walked up them, through the open door into the house.

SIXTY

The interior of the house was dark. The smell was what struck me first, or rather the absence of smell. In spite of the age of the house, the plethora of hard dark wood, the late eighteenth-century portraits which hung on the wall, and faded oriental rugs, there was no musky sweetness, no atmosphere of dust. The absence of smell had a curious effect: it made the interior of the house seem as if it were a backdrop, a fake, a *trompe-l'oeil*. Or a three-dimensional phantom that only appeared to have substance. I put my hand out to touch the bottom whorl of the oaken staircase.

Justine was somewhere in here. She was waiting for me to come to her rescue, at the top of the house, in the room with barred windows. There were no signs of life down here in the hallway. Neither were there any signs of the presence of her abductor. The main hall began to appear to me more like a stage set for some melodrama. But I knew that the reality of Justine was imprisoned somewhere above me, the soft voluptuous reality of her. Making love to her would be a consummation of the weeks that had led up to it, all the pain and design. My desire, once consummated, would justify reality. Or rather give back reality to what I saw around me. It would make life real.

I called out her name.

It hung in the air, seemed to mark the place and space in time. But there was no reply. I felt strangely unafraid. The abductor was obviously out of the house. It was all falling into place.

I made my way up to the top floor. I walked along the corridor, softly, to the room from where I had seen Justine look down at me, between its bars. However, to my surprise, the door was wide open. The small bare room was empty except for a pen and some sheaves of paper lying on a wooden table and a chair. The light fell in exactly the same way as it had in the background to the portrait of Justine. But Justine was no longer in the painting. Entering the room, I walked up to the window and looked out through the bars. Formal gardens reached out from the back of the house, tapering out into the smooth flat plains of wheat fields.

The door slammed shut behind me and a key turned in the lock. I ran up to the door and frantically pulled at the handle. The door was made of thick solid oak.

'What the hell do you think you are doing?' I shouted through it.

I had no idea who I was talking too, but I heard the sound of his footsteps recede into silence.

I looked around again at the desolate room. It was small and stuffy. I sat down at the table. The walls were blank.

SIXTY-ONE

As I write now, I cannot really remember in any great detail my reaction to being locked in. It was as if, because I had visited the house before in my dream, that what was happening to me at the time was also unreal. All I knew was that it was my Destiny to rescue Justine. I was not afraid. As I write now, I realize more clearly that my reaction was really one of feeling that I had been set a test.

I tried the window. It opened easily but the bars behind it were unbreakable. I had expected them to be as old as the house but to my surprise they were shiny new. Someone had designed this prison for me very recently. There was no leverage with which to jolt the door open.

I knew it was important to retain a sense of control over my circumstances. Thinking in long, well-con-structed sentences helped me maintain a sense of power over these events. The blank paper and the pen stared suggestively up at me from the table. A message – I was supposed to write a message. But to whom? The room was absent of clues and the situation reminded me of Juliette's flat after it had been abandoned.

I went to the window again and looked out over the

garden. I could see from above clearly the symmetrical pattern of the maze. From up here the design was easy to read. A bench had been placed in the centre of the maze. On the bench, in the early evening, a woman was sitting reading. It was Justine. The abductor must have imprisoned her in the centre of the maze. But a few moments later the woman stood up and calmly began to make her way out of the maze, following its twisting configurations unerringly, as if she had known its secrets since a child. The exit was directly below my window and I could see her more clearly as she approached the end of the maze's long corridor. I noticed the ill-fitting clothes she was wearing, the way she walked slightly defensively, the way she looked straight up at me, in my direction, but didn't register what she saw. It wasn't Justine. It was Juliette. She disappeared into the house.

So Juliette was *here*. But what was she doing here? Had she been kidnapped too?

Just then there was a knock on the door. A black joke, I thought, I can hardly say come in.

'Who is it?' I asked. My voice sounded odd.

'It's Justine.' She was speaking softly. 'I've managed to get out of my room. He left the key in the lock. But the outer door –'

'I've got to talk to you,' I interrupted. 'There's so much I don't understand. I've just seen *Juliette* in the garden.'

'Don't worry. I'll explain everything to you. But you're going to have to wait. I can hear him coming.'

She fell silent.

'Justine?' But I could hear her footsteps disappearing down the corridor. 'Justine.' JUSTINE.

By the next morning, having spent a night on the hard boards without any food or water, I was becoming desperate. I was not used to any form of deprivation. I started clawing at the door shouting Justine's name over and over again. I was pounding at the door, shaking it, knowing that there was no way I would be able ever to defeat its intractable strength.

SIXTY-TWO

I sat down at the table and picked up a pen. On a blank piece of paper I wrote,

JULIETTE. I'VE BEEN IMPRISONED IN THE ROOM AT THE FAR END OF THE EAST SIDE OF THE HOUSE ON THE TOP FLOOR. THE ONE WITH BARS ON ITS WINDOWS. PLEASE HELP ME.

I signed my name.

I then moved the chair to the window and sat down and waited for her to come out into the garden again.

Early in the afternoon of the next day she appeared, carrying her book. I watched as she entered the maze confidently and weaved her way through into its centre. After an hour of reading she walked out of the maze in the same way. As she was walking underneath my window, I put my hand to the frame to throw out the message. But the window stuck. No matter how hard I pushed upwards, I couldn't get it open. I was too far up for her to hear my cries.

During the night I finally managed to open the window. I was then reluctant to close it in case I could not get it open again. The wind at night was freezing and I slept curled up in the corner of the hard floor. The room was also beginning to smell of urine and excrement. Juliette did not appear the next day nor the next.

I was growing fainter and fainter. If I had been offered food now, I would not have been able to eat it. The pain of my hungry stomach had been replaced by an odd feeling of fullness, as if it had been stuffed with empty space. I began to lose track of the passing time.

I continued my vigil by the window. Early one morning, Juliette finally entered the garden again. Without hesitation I threw the message down to her through the bars of the window.

The paper floated through the air like a butterfly to land by her feet. I watched her bend down and pick it up and read it. I signalled desperately to her between the bars. Her face seemed stony, to give away no response. Suddenly she turned up her face in my direction. The sun came out and I could see the expression on her face more clearly. She was laughing. She was throwing back her head in laughter.

I withdrew into the darkness of my cell and lay curled up on the floor in the foetal position. Now the smells of the room, instead of repulsing me, had begun to offer me comfort. Their acrid warmth had become the proof of my existence.

SIXTY-THREE

I shut the window that night. There was no need to have it open any longer. Was I to remain here until I starved to death? In spite of what I had done for the abductor, for having killed John Baptiste, was I to be rewarded not with Justine but with a slow lingering death? I had been right about Juliette. She was in league with the abductor, unknown to her sister: she had seen me and laughed. Did that make Juliette involved in Jack's death too? Had her desire for revenge taken her that far? Had I been just a pawn employed by her to murder him? But where in all these torturous convolutions did this leave Justine?

I began to wonder if Justine was a monster of my own creation. Locked up in the room I wondered if my imagination had created her all along, that she was just the projection of my obsession made bodily flesh.

She began to take on paranormal qualities: at night she shook the house so it felt like the wind was blowing through. Her presence permeated the house, the sound of a creaking door was the moan of her complaint, the rattling of the glass window her laughter.

I became increasingly aware that my room was only a component of a giant house, a vulnerable locked-away part, while the house with its own machinations went about its gigantic business, with its sounds and rustles. The paranoia increased, and I felt perpetually monitored, perpetually watched by the house that was permeated by Justine.

I began to long for the detail of the rest of the house, of the outside world, outside my small room. The longer I stayed here, the more absent the details of the room became. I knew each crack in the wall so well that they ceased to seem real.

SIXTY-FOUR

One night I dreamt that I heard footsteps coming down the corridor towards my room. The key turns in the lock, but the door remains shut. Footsteps walk back down the corridor. I try to stand up but the chain that binds my leg stops me short. But as I look down the clasp miraculously opens wide to show its smiling teeth. Looking out of the window it is late evening and the full moon is shining outside so brightly it almost seems like day. I can see over the giant wall that surrounds impenetrably the grounds of the house. A huge city stands outside the wall with cars and people. We have been in the heartland of London all along. I look over to the maze where Juliette again sits in the centre. She is reading a book by the light of the moon.

I walk down the stairs into the cool, silent, summer night air. The scent of lavender hangs in the air. I can no longer see over the huge wall that has grown up in my dream, which soars up high around the tapering lawn. The outside world has vanished. The maze now dominates my vision.

I am obsessed by the need to find Juliette. I need to find out what has happened, to strangle the information out of her, so that I can understand finally what is happening to me. This is the pursuit of a knowledge that I know unconsciously I already have. This knowledge is like a cancer that has been proliferating in my body, only able to make itself known to me when it comes to the surface in its own specific shape.

I enter the maze. The hedge looks dark green at night, menacing, but the bright moon gives it a thick dimensionality. Every leaf shines. I walk down a path only to reach the dead end of a hedge. The next path I take is blocked. When the one after that reaches nowhere, I begin to panic, for now I am lost.

It is then that the humming begins. A woman is humming the tune 'Greensleeves'. I follow it through the maze, as if it is a Siren luring me to my death. I turn a sharp corner.

I am now standing in the centre of the maze. On a bench, Juliette is sitting, reading. Engraved on the red leather covering of the book, in gold lettering, are the words *Juliette by the Marquis de Sade*. When she looks up and sees me, she smiles. At the same time she shuts the book.

I run up to her and grab her by her shoulders, the book flies out of her lap on to the ground. I begin shaking her violently.

'Tell me, Juliette,' I say. 'Tell me what is happening to me.'

'But you've made a mistake,' she says to me quietly. I stop shaking her, suddenly frightened by her coolness. 'I'm not Juliette. I'm Justine.'

But her voice, the expression in her face, her posture they are all features that belong to Juliette and my world grows faint.

SIXTY-FIVE

I was woken up from my dream by a scream coming from the distant corner of the house, then the shouting of two women's voices, one higher pitched than the other, one belonging to Juliette the other to Justine. I couldn't work out the words but I could hear furniture being banged and the crashing of china being smashed to the ground. Then silence fell.

I heard footsteps coming down the corridor towards

my room. The key turned in the lock, but the door remained shut. Footsteps walked back down the corridor and quickly afterwards the shouting started up again. I looked down at the chain that bound my leg: to my surprise the chain had gone. But then I remembered, the chain had only been part of my dream. In reality I had never been chained. I cautiously stood up off the floor, my legs unsteady. I pressed the door and it opened easily and silently. The corridor had been lit with the dull blue glow of gas-light. The shouting suddenly became louder and I could hear clearly the words, 'Stop playing these games with him' spoken in the hysterical tone of Juliette. And then the cool relaxed note of Justine's laughter in response. The words were coming from a room a few doors up from me on the left. I could tell that the door was ajar as light was pouring through the chink into the dimness of the corridor. I walked quietly down the corridor and peered round the edge of the door.

Inside was a huge, high-ceilinged room – a four-poster bed framed in crimson old velvet streaked with dust stood in its centre. The painting of Leda and the swan hung on the wall. The carpet was faded to the colour of the walls: an old fawn beige. Books had been flung across the room, their leather bindings split and the pages torn. Pieces of bone china lay scattered across the room.

Juliette was standing to one side of the room, facing in my direction, speaking to the armchair where Justine was sitting. Justine was obscured from my view by the back of the armchair. A candle on the bedside table offered the only light but I could make out enough of Juliette's face to see that the structure was contorted by anger and pain.

'Are you incapable of EXPRESSION? TELL me what you are thinking, Justine. Don't just sit there with your secret cold schemes, leaving me all alone in the dark.'

Juliette lunged for the armchair and for a moment I thought she was going to violently attack Justine. But instead she tore off the arm covers and began ripping up the rose-covered fabric into pieces. They scattered round the room like confetti. Underneath the chair was an intricate structure of wire and hair, like a monstrous piece of machinery.

Juliette turned and started to walk in my direction. She seemed to be looking straight at me, but was still talking to Justine. 'How long are you going to go on with this pretence of being abducted? Inventing phantom characters as if you were writing a book. Using fiction for your own malicious ends.'

Justine did not reply.

So the abductor had just been a fictitious character of Justine's mind. His existence had been a fabrication. I was part of a far larger plot. Justine had not been kidnapped. I had.

I returned unquestioningly, of my own accord, to my room. The fact that the outside world had locked me up only seemed the natural consequence of the inside of my mind. I no longer needed to leave. But to which sister's plan did I belong and to what end? It never occurred to me to wonder that if there had been no abductor, then who had asked me to murder Jack?

SIXTY-SIX

I found out the next day to whose plan I belonged. It was

of course, Justine's. Juliette had never come into the picture. Not really, ever.

On waking, I heard from outside the window the voice of a woman singing.

Alas my love! Ye do me wrong
To cast me off discourteously.
Greensleeves was all my joy.
Greensleeves was my delight,
Greensleeves was my heart of gold,
And who but Lady Greensleeves?

I went to the window and looked out, leaning heavily on the window sill for support. I was too weak from hunger to stand without support. From down below, Juliette was staring up at me, slightly hunched, smiling. As soon as she saw me, she stopped singing. She had been waiting for me. She started to undress.

I watched her coarsely-woven clothes fall off her like leaves from a dying tree. I watched them as if they were falling in slow motion through the air, of their own accord. A wind suddenly rushed through her hair, momentarily concealing her face. A cloud crossed the sun but the shadows only accentuated her expression where the sun previously had blanked out her face. It seemed to take forever until she stood there naked.

She stood looking at me proudly, like a deer that one comes across accidentally in a forest, before it runs off startled. The tone of her flesh in the shadows transformed her flesh from silver into bronze. She looked up and smiled and in her smile was all the awareness of her nude beauty. I felt as if I were flying down to her, that I was not trapped in this room watching from behind barred windows. But what she did next shocked me back into the prison of my body, freeze-framed me back into another reality.

I watched as Juliette slowly got dressed again, not in the same dress, but in an elegant, deep green silk that wrapped itself round her body. She stood up straight and gracefully. The expression on her face had changed. It had become serene and distant. It had become Justine's face. Justine then looked up and smiled at me. I turned from the window.

I noticed for the first time that sometime during the night a bed had been placed in the corner of the room.

SIXTY-SEVEN

Footsteps sounded on the stairs. The door opened and Justine entered. Her face was as smooth as alabaster. She bent down over me where I had lain down on the bare bed and clasped an iron chained ring round the ankle of my deformed foot. She padlocked the chain to the bed. I saw her breasts sway under the dark green silk of her dress.

She stood up above me and looked down without saying anything.

'There are no twin sisters,' I said slowly. 'Or rather they are both you. All along it has always been just you. Just Justine.'

'Did you know that man's ability to manipulate his own kind is what distinguishes him from the other animals? That I manipulated Jack, and then manipulated you in order to wreak revenge on Jack, is what distinguishes me from the lower primates.' She laughed. 'I am a jealous god. You know jealousy too, don't you? I mean know, intimate like a lover, the closeness of jealousy. Been as intimate with it as Christ was with his cross. A cauldron of blood, metal and wood. I have the stigmata too but it is on the inside.

'Juliette fell in love with Jack. But she never trusted him. His eyes consistently strayed. Like the eyes of a lost dog. She decided to set him a test. She invented a sister: Justine. Justine was independent, omnipotent and unable to love. Juliette didn't stand a chance against her. Jack fell. Poor Juliette. But more poor Jack. Jack didn't believe in jealousy but you and Juliette did. That is why trapped between our singular desires he had to die.

'In order to take revenge on Jack I had to be elaborate: I needed a murderer. You came along just at the right time. The image of Justine ensnared you, then Juliette came along to put the trap into operation. Juliette was necessary to give credence to the story of the abductor.'

'But what about the ribbons? Who left those behind?'

'Justine.'

'Who wrote the letters? Those obscene letters?'

'Justine. Juliette knew where you lived, remember.

'But I don't take full credit for the murder of Jack. It was your jealousy of my image that really did it. You wanted your notion of my beauty for yourself. It was not the abductor's threat of my death, but the threat of the death of your fantasy that killed Jack. But the fantasy of the abductor *did* bring you out here. Of course, in your heart you know that *you* are the real abductor. The abductor of Justine's identity. You wanted it for your own. So in the end it's only fair that you are punished too'.

But I was still confused. 'So which one are you? Justine or Juliette?'

'Did either of you really think you could divide me up that easily? Like a child sorting out two colours of brick. But both you and Jack were always one for appearances. While the real me was climbing between the two phantoms of Justine and Juliette, living somewhere in the space between the two and neither you nor Jack noticing, neither of you concerned with who I really was.

'You both really should have guessed, you know. The characterizations were so basic. Omnipotent Justine and needy Juliette, virgin and whore. Just enough to titillate the preconceptions. You were both one of a kind, the murderer and the murderee. It was inevitable in the end that you had to cancel each other out.'

SIXTY-EIGHT

Anger cracked open the hard shell of my obsession. It was as if my heart had been plucked out and swallowed up by the air around me.

'So now you know,' she continued, '*My* story was the real one. I'm not talking about *Death is a Woman*. It never existed. I'm not talking about words on pages, about my failed attempts to get published, about pale representations. I'm talking about the story I have really written, the story of Justine. The story I have got you, my ghost-writer, to write for me. I'm talking about the real thing. I'm talking about the story of life. And the story of death. That's where having a plot really counts. But you chose to ignore *my* story. As have all the men in my life. You were too busy making up your own. If I was to be the heroine of your book, you could at least have given me a speaking part. But now that you have acted out my story, I think it's time that you put it down in writing too.' She paused and smiled. 'Just for posterity.'

For the first time since I had laid eyes on her I wanted out.

But what was the true identity of this woman? I had to call her Justine just to hook on to some kind of reality. I could not cope with more than one illusory woman at a time. Was she insane? How far was she in control of her own actions? How far was she in control of mine?

After she had left the room, I tried to look for signs of madness in the entangled intricacies of our shared history but I was met with a television shut-down of contradictory conversations and information.

She had certainly acted at all times as if she had been in absolute control. She even had her sense of control under control. For had she not acted out the implacable cold image of Justine just as she had acted out the passionate incoherence of Juliette, with equanimity? She was not mad at all. She was simply a woman possessed by a lucid sense of revenge. Hell hath no fury.

SIXTY-NINE

I cherished the fury that her revelations had generated in my heart. My anger was a reclamation of my identity: my rage fought against the world of Justine that I had slipped into, had been slowly sliding into like quicksand from the moment I had first seen her. All along, I had assumed that I had been bringing *her* into *my* world, so that I could put her in a glass case, a private exhibition of her which I could let out at my delectation to taste her sweet flesh. I had been tricked by the beautiful object that I had sought to possess. She had had her own thoughts and desires which had manipulated me. There was a parallel universe and it belonged to her. Worse, she had dragged me into it.

I nursed my anger as I once had nursed my love. My anger felt good, like a long lost friend who made me remember how I once was. The reality of the world around me suddenly took on new meaning again. It became imperative that I escaped.

Justine seemed oblivious or indifferent to the change in my feelings for her. She shouldn't have been, as they were dangerous. In fact, instead of being on her guard she now seemed to relax. It was as if her confession had in some way absolved her. She began bringing me in food every day. I swallowed needily mouthful after mouthful, while she would just watch with cold appraising eyes. She would then take the tray away without uttering a word.

Weeks passed and I slowly began to despair at ever managing to escape. The room was devoid of anything that I might use as a weapon and I still doubted I was strong enough to overpower Justine without one.

One day as I was eating, Justine silently watching me as usual, the sun suddenly came out from behind a cloud and a bright beam shot across the room. With the fluid intuition of a dream, I lifted my head up as if someone had just walked into the room and was standing behind Justine's left shoulder. Uttering a scream, I tried to stand up as if to take a step away, but the chain that bound my leg to the bed pulled me back and the tray and the cutlery fell crashing to the floor. A knife fell at my left foot.

But she didn't turn to look behind. She sat simply staring at me in astonishment, as if I had gone insane.

'Jack,' I said to the phantom standing behind her.

And it was, for a moment, as if I actually did see him standing there.

This time Justine, letting out a cry of shock, twisted her body violently round. For a moment she must have wondered if I had killed Jack at all. Unless she believed in ghosts.

I watched the back of her body relax when she saw no one was there and she turned slowly round again to face me, her expression calm and cold.

'You are having bad dreams,' she said quietly. 'That way madness lies.'

But after she had picked up the tray and left the room, I bent down under the bed and picked up the knife which I had kicked out of sight under it.

SEVENTY

Lunchtime next day came too slowly and by the position of the sun I could tell that Justine was late. Justine was never late. I finally heard her footsteps echo down the corridor. Imprisonment in a room meant footsteps now were always precursors to her presence, were always how she made herself first felt.

It was my turn to play. Possum. I lay down on the bed, my arms dangling over the sides as if I were unconscious. The metal of the knife concealed in my left hand was sticking hotly to the flesh of my palm. I listened to the key turn in the lock and the door open. The sound of her footsteps clipping on the wooden floor as she crossed the room stopped abruptly. I, on the other hand, felt calm in this new black world where Justine had become reduced to a series of arhythmic sounds. I heard her put the tray down on the floor, too loudly. I had unnerved her. Her grandmother footsteps started up again.

Justine's breath smelt of lilies as she bent down over me. *In another world she would have been about to kiss me.*

I swiftly brought up my arms about her neck as if in an embrace. I could hear her inhale sharply in surprise. With my eyes still shut I stabbed her sharply in the side of the neck. I could feel the metal of the knife penetrate the surface of the skin, meet bone. I had expected her to collapse. Instead Justine began to grapple with my body with what seemed superhuman strength. It was as if my action had created a monster.

I opened my eyes to be met with her face bearing down directly above me. It shone with beatific joy. It made her beauty seem demonic. The knife stuck out of the side of her neck like a bolt.

We fell from the bed on to the floor, our bodies intimately intertwined. I screamed out loud as the chain pulled my leg violently and painfully taut. Her body was muscular and powerful, resistant to all my attempts to subdue it. Relentless arms pulled back mine, her legs kicked up into my groin, her head butted into my face, forcing the back of my skull to bang hard against the floor. Pinioned to the floor, I looked up into her clear all-seeing eyes. My eyes slowly filled with tears.

Astride my prone body she stood up to her full height and looked down at me. Reaching up her hand to her neck, with a cursory movement she pulled out the knife.

She didn't flinch. The knife came out unstained – the only trace of a neck-wound was the faint outline of a hole in the shape of a heart.

'That was a mistake,' she said.

She picked up the tray of untouched food and took it out of the room, locking the door behind her. Long after she had gone, I could still hear her footsteps echo down the corridor.

SEVENTY-ONE

Justine didn't return. I lost count of the days that passed without food or drink. The hair that had grown on my face was a source of constant irritation to me, and I constantly scratched at the skin around my beard until my face grew raw and inflamed. I now no longer noticed the smells that emanated from the room or from my armpits and groin.

Soon afterwards the hallucinations began. Not the dreamy/nightmarish hallucinations that I had experienced while opiated but hallucinations that featured scenes from my past, real life events, transposed into the present.

I saw my mother crouched down beside the wall, young and beautiful, diamonds glittering in her hair, smiling comfortingly at me. Lethe would come up to me as I sat at the table, and rub her head against my leg. Part of my room would be transformed into an exact replica of Kensington Gardens, and looking out of the window I would see not the maze, but the square's gardens. I began to look forward to these hallucinations, as a form of nostalgic entertainment, as if they were scenes from a film I had watched as a child.

I woke up one morning to see that the walls had now been papered over in a fine yellow wallpaper. I am sure I saw the patterns on the wallpaper shift. At first I wasn't. Now I am. I could smell the scent first. Of sweet flowers, then I see them growing in paper patterns all over the wall. They are giant red roses with a green intricate filigree of fine leaves. The roses seem too big for the slim stems as if their heads are about to break off their swaying necks. The roses are engorged blood-red, the shadowed crevices between the petals making them look three-dimensional as if they are growing out of the wall, as if their heads are peering out into my small world. The leaves curve out into the shape of a J as if reaching out to an invisible sun. Then the flowers start to change shape. They grow larger and paler, their petals spread out and open, become hooked. The red drains from the petals to leave a bled whiteness, veined by red before the red finally disappears altogether. The roses become lilies which sway in my sleep, which sway through my brain suffocating my thoughts with their heavy perfume.

Sometimes I feel sure that a woman is trying to break through the wallpaper from the outside but then I realize that she already has. She is creeping about the house, like a ghost, haunting me.

That night I dreamt that I saw something moving from behind the wallpaper. I saw the paper protrude in the shape of a naked woman's body before she broke through the paper to reveal herself. It was Justine. She bent down over me, and gently undid my clothing and caressed my weary limbs. Her hands were soft and knowing, as if they had touched me before. She sat astride me and held my arms to the floor above my head and I simply lay there, too enfeebled to move, while she seized her pleasure from me. Her skin shone in the darkness like silver. I came helplessly, while she came loudly, triumphantly. I hadn't touched her with my hands, or kissed her once. Still astride me, she bent down and whispered in my ear,

'*Am I what you imagined?*'

I could hear her still laughing, long after she had slipped back behind the wallpaper.

I woke up, semen sticking to the inside of my thighs. A succubus, I thought, had come to me in the night. Except that I was now naked and my clothes were no longer in the room.

SEVENTY-TWO

The pain in my stomach had come back and in the form of birds trying to peck their way out of my body. I felt a kind of dreary lassitude where the outside world no longer had any power over me. Rather, I was gently slipping out of it. Over the next few days, I lay in my excreta, and urine and blood, watching the bones protrude from my body one by one.

I must have been unconscious for days, the evening Justine finally returned. The noise of the door opening brought me round. When I looked up and saw a woman standing in the doorway I thought at first it was Salome. Justine was wearing a black veil which transparently clothed her naked body. She turned slightly to the door so that I could see the upward sweep of her breasts. I could tell, by the flicker of the smile across her face that she was taunting me. In spite of, or now perhaps because of, my debilitated state I desired her, but it was mixed with a rush of hatred which eroticized her still further. She stood above me so that I could now see the under-curve of her full breasts above me, the pink aureole of the nipple just beginning.

'Kneel,' she said quietly.

With difficulty, as the chain had been shortened, I climbed out of bed and got down on my knees. The skin on my body cracked with the effort. I bowed my head. When I looked up she had gone.

The next day at the same time the same thing hap-pened. Except this time when I knelt and bowed my head, I heard the sound of a whiplash and felt a searing pain slice across the back of my neck. I tried not to cry out loud.

Each day the whippings became more and more severe until my body was a mosaic of cuts and gashes. The area of my body that the whipping covered gradually increased from the neck to the back, to the buttocks and the back of my legs. It hurt to make the slightest movement. My body was in a constant state of bleeding and bruises. The sur-face of my skin had been erased.

I lost all sense of the passing of time. Time just con-sisted of the moments between beatings. I became a body without a soul, that only experienced the ecstasy of pain. I lived in fearful anticipation of the moment when Justine would next enter the room.

I fought against giving in to my obsession for her again with all my heart. Desperately, I hung on to my anger against her. But my anger only reinforced my desire. Powerless to stop it, my rage was slowly diffusing, dripping out of me again like the blood from my body. It was slipping from my grasp. I could feel the bodily warmth of my anger slip from my arms. A cool waterfall of acceptance returned to refresh me, leaving me with the blissful emptiness of surrender. I was left cupping the inanimate coolness of empty space.

SEVENTY-THREE

The need to see my tormentor increasingly deepened. I could not stop longing for her next to appear. Her presence broke the anxiety of waiting for the next punishment. At least when she appeared I knew for certain that pain was about to happen. Better that than the terrible space between when there was no pain to block out my identity. I began to long for her, began to feel safe again when she opened the door.

Justine was using me in the purest way. The moment I gave my identity absolutely over to her was the moment of purest sexual release. The straining carapace of my character had been lifted off to reveal the soft centre of naked existence. I now lived for the pain that she offered me. When she whipped me, when she stroked me, I became her hard whip, her cold hand.

I had finally found a satisfaction that I had never known possible. The surface of the world's beauty, its fine art had become vain symbols, extensions of an identity I once had. They had been trashy plastic ciphers all along. The beauty and art in my life had been replaced by the gestures and cruelties of Justine. All natural interest in the world, including the physical representations of myself — my possessions and objects of art, all material things, my body itself – had disappeared. I now lived only for the sensation of absence.

SEVENTY-FOUR

I was dying. One night, late into the night, I heard the door unlock and someone come in. I was too weak to lift up my head. Justine, holding a candle, walked into my line of vision. In reality she looked lovelier than she had in my dreams. She was dressed in white silk, like a bride. I feebly, automatically, outstretched my arm to her.

If I had reached out to touch her, the edge of my hands would have gone straight through, sunk into the warm gauze of her. She lay at the pit of me where my stomach used to be. She lay at the edge of me where my skin used to feel the warmth of a summer breeze but which was now blocked out to all sensation but her. She lay curled up in my entrails like a snake. She was what remained of my identity, the fragments of my personality consisted of her. She stood, gazing at me.

'Justine,' I said.

She smiled at me.

'Why?' I asked. 'Why out of all the men you must know, did you choose me?'

She shook her head. 'But *you* chose *me*. You saw me once at a funeral. We bumped into each other at the gallery. That was Fate. Never knock Fate. But the rest has always been up to you. I did nothing but present my image to you. Your obsession decided on a reality of its own. And ignored mine. It was this that gave me *carte blanche*. Don't blame me for your inability to read what was *really* going on. Your obsession subsumed my identity. And in this lay your downfall. For *you* are the one that has been finally annihilated. The real victim of your obsession has not been me. It's been you all along. The prison I have made for you, and what I do to you inside it, is the physical manifestation of what you have been doing to yourself. I have simply transformed your obsession into literal truth. I have made your spiritual prison real.'

I looked at her opaque, wide-apart eyes and the soft white skin like recently fallen snow. I looked at her mouth which was like a butterfly in flight. I looked hard into her eyes and I saw the truth. She looked like me, in another world.

She walked out of my line of vision and returned holding an axe in her hand. The blade shone as silver as her skin in the candlelight.

'But, you see, I don't want you walking away.'

She raised it above my ankle. I said nothing. Did nothing. What was there left for me to do?

She said, before bringing the axe down on my leg,

'Don't make the mistake of thinking I am mad. I'm terribly, terribly sane.'

SEVENTY-FIVE

I regained consciousness, bathed, draped in a silk dressing-gown, without pain, in a new room. It was also a room that I recognized. It was the exact replica of my drawing-room in Kensington Gardens, containing the same artefacts, all my books and papers, and decorated in a style identical to the original. Even Lethe was curled up in the corner. From where I was lying on the sofa, I could see, through the doorway of my flat, the stairs that led up to my bedroom. *My whole flat* had been replicated with consummate skill. I realized that this was the place in which I was to spend the rest of my life: a prisoner of Justine, a prisoner of love.

I looked down at my leg. A bandage had been expertly wrapped round the stump of my right foot. My foot had been amputated. Justine had removed my deformity. She had rendered me physically immaculate.

Yet when I looked up at the painting of Justine, I noticed that the figure of Justine was absent from it. The painting of the bare, dark room now seemed devoid of all life: Justine no longer sat at the table which still stood in the centre of the painting and a bed had been placed in the space that she had left. However, on closer inspection, I could just make out the naked figure of a man lying on the bed, his face turned to the wall. The brushstrokes that he had been painted in were blurred and uneven.

Justine was now sitting opposite me in exactly the same position as the original posture of the painting. It was as if Justine had stepped out of the background of the painting, wearing the same velvet dress, into the interior of my Kensington flat. The image of the painting had now literally come to life. She was holding in her hand the book that had once contained pages half covered by her unformed handwriting. However, the book was splayed open now to reveal blank pages, shiny pale pages, devoid of print.

'Who are you?' I asked, suddenly realizing that this was the point to everything, everything I had gone through, the point to the story of Justine.

She paused and looked at me serenely, as if she had just been blessed. She broke into a sudden smile.

'That's for you to find out'. She leant over and handed me the blank book.

She then rose, turned her back to me and walked slowly out of the room.

SEVENTY-SIX

The library is from where I am now writing to you, writing out the story of Justine. I have almost reached the ending. The shadows on the shelves around me are only books. When I hold up their pages to the light, the paper of many of them is so thin that the words on the other side shine backwards, through.